Legran
Le Grange, Jason,
Fanny and Dora's South American
adventure /
$9.99   ocn984694946

Fanny and Dora's South American Adventure

Jason le Grange

~~Lilibeth Llewellyn Rhys-Davies~~

© 2016 ~~Lilibeth Llewellyn Rhys-Davies~~ Jason le Grange

~~Lilibeth Llewellyn Rhys-Davies~~ Jason le Grange asserts ~~her~~ his moral rights to be identified as the author of this book. All rights reserved. No part of this book may be reproduced in any form or by any electronic or mechanical means, including information storage and retrieval systems, without written permission from the publisher or author, except in the case of a reviewer, who may quote brief passages embodied in critical articles or in a review.

Published by Wesmarg Books
Glasgow – Cape Town – Sydney

www.facebook.com/wesmargbooks

Printed at CreateSpace, Charleston, South Carolina

ISBN-13: 9781536806274

ISBN-10: 1536806277

i can't breathe!!!!

Get his nose hairs as punishment for this terrible act, so that i can <u>burn</u> them!

To the wonderful women of this world

and beyond:

Margaret

Nina

Frances

and

Sandy

where is my name? I always dedicate books to myself!!!!

Part One ~
Preparation
or, simply put;
coming to terms with diet-friendly world domination

Chapter One
England
-Small little village

"We need to talk now," the voice was firm and in control, "it cannot wait another minute."

Fanny sighed deeply thinking of her unfinished *Sudoku* and conceded graciously, "Alright then."

Fanny had lived in the small English village her whole life. She had watched the children move to the bigger towns. She had listened to her trusty radio as Prime Minister after Prime Minister had come in and out of Downing Street. She even remembered the Second World War and yet with all this action she felt her village had weathered the storm and always remained a dignified place to live.

So what was the crisis going to be now? Another bazaar to organise? The Vicar's birthday party? Surely, not another one of those awful bingo evenings? A small shiver crept through Fanny's body as she remembered the humiliation of having to dress up as an Inuit and select the Bingo numbers by 'fishing' with a magnetic cord. She couldn't suffer that ordeal again.

There were two sharp military-like rings of the doorbell. Fanny could hear herself taking in an extra deep breath of air. She always seemed to have this reaction when only one person rang the doorbell: Dora Pembury.

Fanny thought she could just pretend she was not there, but then she remembered she had just taken the call. Reluctantly, she edged herself closer to the door handle, accepting that if she didn't open the door now, another series of rings would ensue. Fanny eased the lock and took another deep breath.

The locals had always made fun of Fanny and Dora. Fanny was a hearty woman who could easily put back a good cream tea. She always dressed as if she was going to lunch with the Queen and took great care in presenting herself correctly. Dora was quite different. She was overly tall and liked to tower over people in more ways than one. She had many nicknames in the village but one she didn't know -- and everyone else did – was Matron Dora. She knew everything about everyone and if there was dirty laundry to air, Dora would be the first to take the most moral high ground.

Standing together, Fanny and Dora looked like Laurel and Hardy, only more comedic, as Dora was tall, and Fanny was round!

Dora marched into the hallway and without breaking her stride declared, "Some tea would be lovely."

Fanny rolled her eyes, making sure 'no one' (Dora!) could see her, and then mumbled under her breath and in a distant whisper, so that 'no one' could actually hear her, "Lovely to see you too."

In no time two cups of tea and slices of banana bread were presented very professionally on a tray.

Without even acknowledging the detail, Dora looked Fanny straight in the eye and said, "I have so much to say and I simply don't know where to start. But Fanny, I implore you to consider this seriously."

Fanny felt the bottom of her stomach roll out and roll right out of the house in pure anxiety.

Dora continued, "Fanny, you know my nephew John; the one with that Asian 'best friend'."

Fanny smiled dutifully, displaying at least some of her teeth. Dora continued without waiting for an answer. "Well, he and his 'best friend' have just completed a most engaging South American holiday."

It came to Fanny; they were going to have to either hold a church bazaar or fête for the starving children of some obscure South American country. Oh dear, she thought. Would this mean dressing up in carnival clothing and parading through the streets while people threw apricots at them? How she wished for a simple life.

"Fanny, are you fading?" Dora commanded, and this required Fanny to flash her teeth once more into a smile and to nod, which looked more like a spasm in execution.

4

"Well, he and his 'best friend' sent me a few postcards and it simply looked wonderful."

Fanny thought she'd better say something at this stage or she might be reprimanded. "How delightful," she tutted, "such caring boys."

"Yes, aren't they," Dora acknowledged, actually taking a moment to breathe. "Anyway, so this got me thinking..." Dora exclaimed, and in an almost breathless statement continued, "…well…well…well…"

Fanny was most concerned that Dora may have a seizure if she continued like this. However, what concerned her much more was what hair-brained event she would be forced into planning.

"I'm getting completely out of breath about all of this," Dora said and she fell back into the Queen Anne armchair decorated so classically with a tartan cushion that Fanny could not help admiring. "I will simply have to come out with it. My nephew and his 'best friend' said that they had not used a travel agent but rather the Internet and some books."

"I thought the Internet was a haven for paedophiles and gamblers?" Fanny enquired. "Isn't that what the Vicar said in a sermon last year?"

"Probably did," Dora muttered, "but it can be a very helpful resource."

"Have you used it?" Fanny asked doubtfully.

"As a matter of fact, Fanny, there is a lot that has happened in the last three weeks that I would never have normally done."

Dora was upright again, banana bread in one hand and tea cup in the other gesticulating wildly, which caused Fanny to panic as she did not wish to remove tea and butter stains before the meeting of the Women's Association tomorrow.

"Fanny, I have done the most amazing things, things I thought I would never dream of in the last weeks. Once you understand it all you are going to simply explode."

The tea ventured partly outside the tea cup but, in true Dora style, magically landed safely back inside.

Dora mechanically placed the banana bread in her mouth and chewed quickly to get it out of the way.

"Fanny, I placed an inter-library loan for a book called 'Internet for Dummies'; obnoxious, I know, but it unlocked a whole world for me. I feel like Pandora's Box has been opened and I'm like whoever that fellow was with the forty thieves."

"Ali Baba," Fanny interjected.

"Yes, yes…that's the one. Well, in this short time I have set up an e-mail account, ordered a book through Amazon.com and joined a chat group on MSN Groups."

Fanny looked at her friend across the room not quite knowing what to say, and in order to fill what was about to because an uncomfortable silence. "You ordered a book from the Amazon? How interesting."

"Not *the* Amazon, Fanny, an online shop called Amazon, where you can shop for anything you want and have it delivered to your home."

Fanny smiled and surmised that Dora was probably not taking her medication. Poor lamb, she sometimes needed medication for her migraines. Maybe she was in so much pain that she had become delusional. None of what she was saying made any sense. Amazon and e-mail could be French as far as she was concerned.

"Do you have a headache, dear?" Fanny asked diplomatically.

"Fanny, there is nothing wrong with me. I haven't felt this good since Prince Charles remarried."

Dora leaned dangerously forward and looked her straight in the eyes. Fanny was thankful she had recently been to the bathroom, because that look could have caused an accident.

"Fanny, you are my best friend and I have to just come out and say it. I want us to go on an overseas holiday together. Money is no object; after all, we can't take it with us, right?"

Chapter Two
England
-Small little village but with some minor issues

Fanny would have loved to say that she was looking forward to a trip abroad with Dora but that would be as far apart and as deep as the English Channel.

Fanny recalled the look of sheer delight on Dora's face after mentioning a trip together; her eyes were alight, her voice was fiery, her spirit soared. This was in direct contrast to how she had felt. Fanny remembered losing feeling in her entire body and having to pinch herself really hard to bring herself back into the reality of the conversation.

It was a simple reflex, like spitting after brushing your teeth, when Dora had said, "Can I count on you then?"

It might have come out as, "Yes…" but it was not what she was thinking. In fact she was saying, *Hell no! So very very sorry, I have to have my ears waxed.*

It was only much later, after she had closed the door, that she realised the magnitude of what she had just agreed to.

Well, Fanny thought, there must be a way to get out of this. It isn't definite until the bookings are made, so I have nothing to worry about. A few days and then she would drop a remark about not being able to go; the reason would come in good time.

Fanny was not going to be confined to Dora for a two-week trip to the Americas. It was just not humanly possible. Or rather it simply wasn't humane.

To Fanny's absolute horror, what she thought was a two-week holiday, controlled, to one single country, the Americas, was in fact going to be a six-week episode – not to New York City where the Americans lived, but to a series of countries to which she had not ever deemed the need to visit.

After all, is that not what musicals are for? Wasn't there that musical about Evita, who saved the country from the 'baddies' and then sang 'Don't Cry for me Argentina' from the balcony as the people below wept in absolute gratitude? There was therefore no reason to visit, as all you needed to know about the country came from watching Madonna sing (and perform) on the screen while spending the country's entire budget on her outfits. One should visit Italy or Switzerland or a place where at least they understand the value of the Pound, but countries in another hemisphere, another world -- it was just too much. She felt herself breaking out into a mild sweat and could feel her breathing increase.

As she looked in front of her, she could swear Dora was now sitting at her dining room table, with a map of the Americas in front of her, using a pencil to point out where they would be visiting in theory and marking them with little pink Post-It's.

"So there you see, Fanny, we will visit four countries over six weeks and get a taste for all that is South American." With that she did a kind of twirl of her pencil as if it was a magic wand and she had the power to conjure up some weird spirit that would magically make it happen.

It was not a mirage, it was in fact Dora, at her dining room table. How did she get in? Fanny panicked and quickly got up, "Tea? Yes, that's a good idea, tea."

She busied herself making tea and returned armed and ready to say, *Thank you for calling, your call is important to us...but I can't go with you, I am pregnant with an illegitimate child.*

Dora had now unpacked a small rain forest onto her dining room table. Fanny placed the two cups of tea and banana bread down in a small corner which had not been consumed by the papers and the books.

"So, this is what we are going to review today. Every day we have reading and research to do."

"Dora..." she began.

"Now, this is not going to be a tick-tick exercise for every damn site in the entire South America. I repeat, we do not have to see everything, but we should at least know our options..." she carried on, despite the interjection.

"Dora...!" this time with a little more volume.

"Yes, Fanny?" she didn't even look up as she said it.

"Well, um...um...."

"Well, spit it out!" Dora commanded.

"Milk?" Her mouth continued to betray her. That was not what she wanted to say, she wanted to pull out of this insanity. Instead she asked about milk, my word!

"You know I have milk." It wasn't said in a hostile manner, more like a typical response to a child that is overbearing.

"Yes...Good," she continued in character, "just checking."

"Now I have selected four countries in total to visit over the six weeks, giving us a taste – a rather delightful and adventurous taste of the jewels of South America. That is what my nephew John did, he said it was perfectly manageable and that they, meaning him and that Asian 'best friend' of his, got to truly experience the different sections of lower South America. Obviously we can't go around the whole of South America in this time, but we can try and do these four, and who knows, we could go back and see the rest in the next trip." She looked up and breathed out.

With more determination this time Fanny took in a deep breath, eased her shoulders back, looked over to where Dora was flicking her pencil in the air and said, "You can never have too many hats, shoes, bags and countries to visit."

Once again Fanny sat back in shock. That was not what she had just instructed her mouth to say. It should have said, *No, Dora, No. Can't do it. I'm afraid the doctor thinks I should rest over the next few months, have a weak nose you know.*

Dora did not even respond. She held up the map and using her pencil as a magic wand, flicked it over the four countries, each time exclaiming the name as if she was summoning up Elvis Presley from the afterlife. "We start our journey in Brrazzzilll, then off to Argentina, followed by an overland passaagggee to Chhillleeeeeeeeee, then a quick visit to the Easter Islands before finishing off in Peruuu."

Fanny already knew she was losing her marbles, by her lack of being able to engage, but the only thought that was buzzing around her head came out of her mouth, unceremoniously, she felt, "And when are we going to Las Vegas?"

Dora looked at her, then tilted her head at a 90-degree angle and said, "Fanny, Las Vegas is in the United States, not in the itinerary this time, but would be happy to consider it another time."

"Right, then, we are going to be eating chillies and having Easter eggs then." Fanny spurted and then smiled the now famous smile and drank her tea while forcing in as much banana bread as she could physically fit into her mouth. Banana bread, she needed to bake more banana bread.

Viva Las Vegas she thought.

Chapter Three
England
-Small little village, in terrifying slow motion

Fanny found herself seated at the bridge table, being treated like a local celebrity. People were fawning over her as if she had recently won the lottery.

"You are so brave," Mrs. Lickett chuckled while touching her on the shoulder. "Women of our age are not explorers or adventurers, but you and Dora...so...brave."

If Fanny thought she was ever going to be famous, it would have been for the banana bread and not the fact that she was going on a kamikaze mission to hell because she couldn't say no.

"Travelling to France is enough of an adventure for me and then I know I am a few hours from home, in case of an emergency, but South America, how very exotic." Mrs Lickett continued, "And over Christmas and New Year when you should be home with your family and friends, to be on your own, hmmm…"

Fanny was hyperventilating and the only source of calm came not from her baked goods, but Marks and Spencer's bought shortbread. At least if her mouth was stuffed full it could not say anything and full was something she was quite capable of.

Dora wasn't able to come to bridge as she had to liaise with her various 'role-players' in the different countries. How vigilant in her pursuit of adventure.

Mrs. Smith, the vicar's wife, looked at her in admiration, not saying a word. She looked back chewing, chewing and then chewing some more.

Mrs. Lickett wasn't finished, "When you return, you simply must have an evening when you show us your slides and share your anecdotes."

Mrs. Smith quickly replied, "This has already been arranged, Dora's booked the Church... I think the hall for two days when they get back. Haven't you been invited?" It was a poke at Mrs. Lickett and a silence ensued, which indicated that she hadn't yet been.

As if to make her point, Mrs. Smith smiled at her in a rather patronising way, cleared her throat and then continued to stare at Fanny.

"Fanny, I can't believe the number of countries you are going to cover in such a short period of time, not to mention that Dora said you are going mostly overland and using the local transportation. In all of those unsafe and lawless places...you...you are an inspiration."

This was the first Fanny was hearing of this, not that she listened to Dora anymore, but public transportation, danger, these were not things she was willing to explore.

Not to be outdone, Mrs. Lickett sat back dramatically and said, "I heard from my sister that a child that goes to university with my niece was robbed and left destitute from a bus they had caught from Edinburgh to London."

There were gasps from all around the room. Followed by some, "Oh, no's..."

Fanny found her face plastered with that smile, she could have been a politician at this rate because what she really felt or wanted to say, was not what came out from the front of her mouth. She was so lost for words at this point, and the shortbread plate was empty, that she found herself taking the piece that rested so gingerly on Mrs. Lickett's saucer. It was in her mouth before anyone even noticed.

"Well that is hardly South America," Mrs. Smith responded.

"Well, if it can happen in Edinburgh, it can happen anywhere." This was accompanied by the look of death.

Lucky for all of them, they were called back to the bridge by a stopwatch which regulated their break time and they were all very competitive so a hasty silence took hold of the room.

Chapter Four
England
-Small little village, but now focus – major crisis!

It looked like a suitcase, smelt like a suitcase and tasted like a suitcase. Alright, she had not tasted the damn thing, but it sure as hell was a suitcase. Not only was it a suitcase, but it was a small one. It had four wheels, supposedly very light, but all of this was immaterial to her, as the problem was that, although she could no longer deny she was going to the Americas, this thing wouldn't even house her toiletries, let alone her clothes.

"Now I can see, Fanny," although Dora wasn't even looking at her, "You are saying with your face, that you doubt that everything could fit into this suitcase. It's best to travel light with the bare minimum. John, my nephew, said that you travel light so that you don't have to check your luggage in. This way, you are always in control of your luggage, can quickly transfer and get around and only have to worry about the other parts of travel. What sensible advice, he really is such a clever boy."

"I see," she heard herself say.

"And let's be clear, crystal clear, crystal clear, …we are not going to buy silly little items in each place we visit, simply for the sake of it. That would mean we would need to take enough luggage to sink the Titanic. No, we are packing light, and if you really see something that you like, and with my expresssss permission only, you can then ship it back here."

Fanny did not say a thing. She simply looked ahead and smiled.

"So, why don't we consider what we should take?" This was not really a question; it wasn't even a casual remark, it was an order. "It's going to be summer, or at least the start of summer, so we only need light clothes. I am even going to suggest one or two skirts, t-shirts -- yes, I don't own any either -- and the odd blouse for when we have a wicked night out."

The last part was obviously a joke because Dora chuckled or snorted and laughed, issuing a sound that could only be described as a vacuum cleaner stuck in a vat of glue.

"Right, then," she replied.

"So, let's pack; make a list of what you still need and then we can organise a quick visit to the shops on the weekend."

Her closets were opened with a military precision, the correct items extracted, while she looked on in morbid fascination. What amazed her the most was that Dora knew where every item of clothing was kept, even what drawer to go into to extract her lighter jerseys. Fanny was not asked for any input, not that she would have been much help.

All the items were then folded, with even more military precision, and placed into said suitcase, proving the point that if you want to go around the Americas half-naked, you can do this by hardly packing any clothes. There was a small amount of space on the top, which she could at least try and force some other things into when Dora was not looking.

Dora, sensing this act of defiance, stated, "Well there you are, all you need are four t-shirts, your toiletries and Bob's your uncle."

"My uncle's name is Richard, not Bob," she said, hypnotised.

"Yes, yes..." Dora took another look at her and then exclaimed, "...why wait for the weekend to get the t-shirts and other stuff? Let's get them now, live dangerously!"

Fanny was about to protest when she found herself being escorted out of the house and into Dora's car which was parked outside. The lanes of the village passed by and within twenty minutes they were in the parking lot of the local department store.

"No time like the present," Dora said, flinging open the car door and nearly knocking a fellow shopper out in the process.

Fanny ran after her like a little child, while Dora marched ahead towards the oncoming automatic doors.

Like before, she just stood there while others around her measured and rotated her and told her what she needed for a 'little extra figure' and then there were four t-shirts in her hand.

They were then in the toiletries section and again Fanny wanted to protest, as she had toiletries at home. "These damned regulations which only allow a few 100ml bottles. Well, I will win in this war, so here are all the little bottles for travel purposes…Don't just look at them, decide which ones you will need."

Fanny looked in front of her and selected what she could, with Dora inspecting each one as if they were auditions and only the best could get through to the next round. Dora, when satisfied, gave a cursory nod to Fanny to follow her. Dora also had her four and they each paid for their own and Dora pulled out a large piece of paper with "TO DO LIST" written on it, and with a focused attack, scratched through item number 3, which said "T-SHIRTS."

Fanny tried so hard to see what the other items were, but the list was quickly put away and then she was in the car and on the way home.

The t-shirts were opened, smelt and declared fit for human wearing without a wash then packed into the remaining space.

"I need a plastic packet, the type you use for freezing vegetables," Dora instructed.

"I don't freeze…" but before she had finished, Dora had marched to the kitchen, found a sealable plastic bag and the toiletries were packed inside.

"All done, so now, to make sure nothing goes wrong, I am going to seal this with a small lock, which I will keep the keys to." With that, she locked the bag and disappeared.

Dora stood in her bedroom staring at the suitcase and trying to piece together all that had happened in the last two hours. She oddly felt a terrible rage towards that John boy, whom she wanted to squash into the newly bought suitcase along with his Asian 'best friend' and send to the Americas as checked-in luggage!

She wanted to recount the events to Mrs. Lickett but realised that there was no way she would believe her. This entire story, as it was unfolding, was getting more and more stranger and 'strangerer' (it is a real word thingie- now focus, please) and on a few occasions she had to make sure that the tea she was drinking had no chemical additives, the ones that made you feel like you were a fairy or a spaceman, or a rock singer. There was a locked suitcase on her floor, she was going to the Americas and -

Doris Day worked mostly at night.

Chapter Five
England
-Heathrow

Fanny had to pinch herself; well no, she didn't, because she was quite aware that she was alive and dragging a suitcase with four wheels across an airport.

Three hours ago she had been saying goodbye, as if she was Sir Walter Scott or those people on those television shows, who are going to have their houses redone and leave the world as they know it behind them. In fact, the whole village had turned out to say goodbye and wish them well on their journey.

There had been a big 'Von Boyage' banner, not that she knew what 'Von' meant, or 'Boyage' for that matter. Dora had corrected her a few times and insisted it was "*Bon Voyage*", but Fanny had not lost all of her senses. If the phrase was French, as Dora had lectured, then it would not be Von, as Von must be linked to German words; the French, on the other hand, liked to roll their tongues across their mouths looking for lost food particles, so the word had to start with the letter B. Logic, why couldn't people just use logic?

For the occasion, they were each wearing a matching t-shirt with the words '*Fanny and Dora's South American Extravaganza*,' boldly printed across it in big black letters. There was a picture of Dora on the left and Fanny on the right. The pictures were cut-outs from the last bazaar when they had taken photographs for the church newsletter. It was disturbing to be wearing yourself!

People came to hug her or squeeze her arm or simply whisper words of encouragement in her ear. It was a show, as people lined up to say their good-byes. She even eyed that insurance man who had sold them the travel insurance, not to mention every other insurance she had, skulking around the periphery hoping to profit off them until the bitter end.

What had made it interesting, if not downright frightening, is that throughout the ordeal she had smiled. It had been automatic, and no matter how she felt inside, her exterior protruded that of a dirty, scandalized politician who had secretly robbed the poor and used drug money to pay for plastic surgery. At one point she even caught a glimpse of herself and could hear an internal conversation taking place (the voice needs a deep raspy tone and the Italian accent): *So, you listen to me scumbag, I know everything about the money, I kill you, I kill you dead...* Only to be transported back into reality and noting that her mouth had not moved an inch, it was still home to the perfect smile.

"You are simply the picture of calm," Mrs. Lickett had said.

"If you say so, dear." She had not actually said this aloud as Dora was the one doing all the talking and she found herself nodding along.

During the big send off, Dora had even raised her hands like that Madonna lady and everyone had laughed and clapped. All Fanny wanted to do was scream out, *I have to be with her by myself for the next six weeks. If you don't hear from me in one day, call the police, send in the Royal Guard, save me!...* The smile remained; it would seem this action was going to be her companion, as much as the pop singer impersonator on the other side of the road.

Dora had arranged for the vicar, Mr. Smith, to drive them. Before she knew it, she was dragging that damn suitcase along the airport pathway. There was the line for the check-in and their suitcases had passed the critical cabin luggage test -- whatever that was. The check-in agent regretted asking about their journey, as Dora extracted the map and itinerary that she had prepared.

Then it was the X-ray machine which kept making obscene beeping noises only for the agent to ask her if she was carrying anything illegal on her person.

"Which person?" she had asked, "There is only Dora and myself."

The agent had eyed her with suspicion and before she knew it, there were hands all over her body. She had screamed in shock, which had in turn caused quite a commotion. Dora stuck into them and, with a look of defeat, they let her through, but continued watching her. She knew this because she kept looking backwards in case they tried any of that funny business again.

Dora navigated the way as they weaved through the people, the shops, the restaurants and the really large number of screaming children contained in one single space and eventually landed up at the gate where their flight was due to board. They waited in silence for half an hour, both exhausted with the activities of the day. Finally, the call came through the loudspeaker, "Ladies and Gentleman, the flight to Sao Paulo, Brazil, is ready for boarding. Could all passengers make their way to Gate B4, please? Thank you."

They both stood up and looked at each other. What happened next left her gasping for air. Dora turned to her, and in a voice as loud as the Grand Prix said, "Fanny, thank you for this wonderful opportunity; it is going to be fun." This was followed by a large bear-like hug, one which was a first. In all the years that she had known Dora (and everyone in the village would agree), she was not a hugger. Her arms remained outstretched as she was unable to move. It took that look from Dora to bring her back to reality, along with the words, "Come along then."

Chapter Six
Country Location Unknown
-Does a plane count as a little village?

It was the closest Fanny could imagine to the birthing process. Unluckily or luckily for her, depending on who you spoke to, she had never met that 'special one' and had not gotten married, nor had children. The pain she was experiencing at this time was so intense that she thought she might cry out aloud. Dora did not seem to be suffering the same as her, for her eyes were fixed on the tiny, yes, really small, screen in front of her watching some troll-like people wandering around the mountainside. Fanny was in such pain, it was simply unimaginable.

It had started a few minutes after she had squashed her lady-like frame into a chair that had clearly been designed for pygmies or the troll-like people that inhabited Dora's screen. To put it politely, she had puffed out on all sides of the chair and had left her legs squashed against the seat in front of her. Once the gypsy-looking infidel in front of her had reclined his seat, she thought she was entering the birth canal backwards. Being so compact, all of the one million hours that they were going to be in flight meant that she was preparing for a personal challenge – which was going to require the patience of an ox, or of a birthing mother who had just learnt that there were another three up there that had not been picked up on the scan.

The meal was served and this required her to be ambidextrous as she wiggled her body in order to accommodate the tray that that air hostess had wedged into her ribs. To say she ate her meal would be a lie because she was hardly able to squash down the salad, let alone the chicken or the one centimetre of chocolate mousse. The tray was whisked away and she was left once more with the throbbing pain in her body.

Fanny looked left and right and then, when she couldn't take it anymore, decided that she would have no choice but to recline too. This meant pushing a button somewhere, so her fingers eased over the remote thingy and she found herself pressing buttons. The first one switched on the television and a picture of Africa emerged, with a lion chasing down one of those fluffy other animals before ripping it into pieces, all in slow motion. The image flashed on the screen about a hundred times. Fanny could feel herself losing consciousness and luckily for her, at the last minute before possibly taking her last breath, she pushed the buttons again and the picture dissolved off the screen.

She continued pushing and was met with a series of flashing lights. "Bloody hell," she heard the words escape her mouth. She didn't know what upset her more, the bad language or the ongoing barrage of light. The kind-looking man sitting next to her reached over and exhumed the remote control from her hands.

"What are you trying to do?" he asked, with a voice not trying to mask the irritation that it felt.

Right then, the smile, the teeth, the diplomat, "Trying to recline my seat."

"Well then, don't touch this, don't touch it at all." He pointed to the silver button on the side of her seat and barked, "Press it in!"

She did as she was told and felt herself sliding backwards and when she felt that she had reclined to the max, she was back in the same position, sitting upright, only to go back down again.

"Let go of the button once you are down," she heard as her face scanned the roof of the plane as she descended once more.

Again she obeyed, lying there having flashbacks to the dentist chair. Now that she thought about it she was in as much panic in the plane, in this chair, as she was when she visited the dentist.

Dora had not glanced once at her during this ordeal, completely transfixed by the screen and that story of the little people in front of her. She couldn't see as clearly anymore as she had when she was sitting up, but she did have a quick look over and she could see those little people were being chased by some kind of jewellery accessory.

Fanny wondered what she had gotten herself into. What were the next few weeks going to do to her sanity? Would she survive? If not, as per the insurance schedule, would they really repatriate her body back to England? Really?

If this was a time for freedom, then it was also time to start using bad language, "Bloody hell." With that she closed her eyes, looked up and thought:

At least I am doing this for England.

Part Two ~
Life is like a box of coffee beans,
or simply put:
every day is a carnival, dahlink!

Chapter Seven
Brazil
-Sao Paulo

Fanny woke up in a cold sweat. Panic had ripped through her entire body and what had made it worse, was that in her dream she kept hearing a man shout, *Don't touch it*, then louder and louder, *don't touch it, push the silver button.*

She looked up at the digital clock next to her bed and the time registered as 4:00 in the morning. She was wide awake and her worst nightmare seemed to be coming into reality. The horrors of jet lag that she had heard about from the Pastor's wife seemed to be very real. "Bloody hell…" She was not sure if she had said it aloud or just thought it; well, there was no one in the room to validate it, so she collapsed back into the pillows, hopeful that this too would pass.

This, however, was not to be the case, as she tossed and turned, rolled and even did a swimming movement in the bed, but nothing helped and it was clear that this was not going to be an opportunity for more sleep.

When she met Dora in the breakfast room, she must have felt like the plate of pork sausages felt, quite dead.

"Well Fanny, you are not looking well," Dora cautioned, but the face did not show any sympathy.

"It is that horrid jet lag that Mrs. Smith spoke of. I've been unable to sleep since practically the moment I lay down. It has been simply horrible."

"Well that is unfortunate," is all that came in response while Dora packed her eggs mechanically into her mouth.

Fanny was expecting some pity, at least a fake murmuring of something, but alas, this was not going to be. She was about to excuse herself from the table, get a taxi to the airport and transport herself back home, when Dora pulled out a paper and laid it on the table.

"Right, so these are my notes for Sao Paulo." She placed her glasses on her nose and peered at the paper with a frown that could have accommodated the Suez Canal crossing, the furrows were so deep.

"Dora…" she began.

"Right, well, I have already said right, but I will say it again, there is no time to dilly-dally today as we have a lot to cover, not to mention our plans for the evening."

Fanny looked around, hoping that someone else dining in the breakfast room would notice that she had been kidnapped and was being held against her will; but alas, all she got was some crazy-looking man who could have been any one of those odd people from one of those even odder Scandinavian countries looking around aimlessly, clearly a victim of jet lag too.

"So we will start with a brisk walk through the Avenida Paulista, not that either of us are shoppers, but the guide book suggested it helps to get a feel of the city."

All Fanny could think of was the phrase 'brisk walk,' because before she could help it the words escaped, "Bloody hell."

Dora looked up surprised, "What was that?"

"Well, yes…I was saying yes… it's warm like the boardwalk of hell," she really needed to understand where these phrases came from that popped out of her mouth.

Dora looked convinced and carried on with the morning lecture. "After that we are going to visit the Museum of Contemporary Art, after which we will have a late lunch in the Liberdade area before retiring to the hotel for an afternoon rest. Tonight, it's drinks and dinner at a hotel that looks like an upside down watermelon. My nephew John and his 'Asian friend' loved it, said it was very glamorous and reminded them of the eating spots in London."

As quickly as the paper had been extracted from the cavernous bag it was replaced and she was left staring at Dora. The mouth did its thing and filled the empty silence with, "Well I don't see a church on the itinerary for today."

Dora took in a deep breath, the brow allowed yet another ship to cross the channel, and she looked at Fanny intensely. "Well I assumed that if you wanted to go somewhere in particular, you would have raised it in the planning phases."

Fanny was bust, but her mouth quickly came to the rescue, "I didn't say we had to go to a church, it's just that on one tour of Scotland I went on..., um... we visited the church first in every town we came across…"

"Precisely, but now I have a question for you. Did you know which church you were going to visit? More importantly, had you read up about the church before you visited. Did you?"

Fanny didn't have to think about this, she rather grumpily agreed that Dora was right, she hadn't known about any of the churches she was going to visit. She was about to say this when she was interrupted yet again by Dora, "I knew it, I knew you hadn't! What I didn't want on this trip is a feeling that we have to go somewhere just because it's in a guidebook, no! We are rather going to spend our time doing the things that sound interesting."

Dora looked at her for a response and the teeth placed themselves into her mouth, as the smile took over.

"I don't want you to think that I am controlling the itinerary, which I technically am, but there is a limited amount of time in each city, town, and river we are going to navigate and I don't want us to have to try and be overly ambitious and lose out because we are chasing attractions."

Fanny felt like shouting out, *Yes, Major!* but bit her lip hard to make sure she did not, thinking about what Dora had just said, actually made sense to her.

"Anything else you would like to add to the itinerary?" Dora's tone concluded that discussion.

"Right then, it's time to leave." With that Dora stood up and walked out. Fanny looked on in horror as she had not even started on her eggs. "Bloody hell!"

'Brisk walk' makes it sound like they sauntered down the Avenida Paulista looking in the shop windows, having a laugh while they looked at something unusual. 'Brisk walk' by Dora's definition would be better suited for a military camp at which navy seals that were going to take down the dictator of the most evil country in the world were being trained. Dora marched in a perfect straight line, with passers-by and other pedestrians scattering at the oncoming tsunami. Fanny would have liked to say that she marched, but that would be problematic; she waddled. She had to come out with it and admit that she waddled like a duck, pregnant with the offspring that would feed every French restaurant in the whole of England. She gasped, she sweated, and yet on they went, making sure they had covered every square inch of the Avenida Paulista. What was that about not having to tick off each attraction?

By the time they arrived at the Museu de Arte de São Paulo she had been reduced, literally, to a sweaty mess, and she found a resolve inside her and demanded, "Water…rest…no movement…now!"

"Right," Dora said and they went into the museum's cafe and sat down and ordered drinks.

A small river, probably the Mississippi, was now flowing out of Fanny and she realised that she was not 'glowing,' the polite term associated with perspiration that she had been taught. She was sweating like a bucket.

During the entire episode Dora watched, as if she was observing a wild animal at a zoo. She was waiting for her to make notes, but she didn't.

After fifteen minutes, life came back to Fanny and she feared that they would be off again, so she made sure to gulp down as much liquid as she could.

"I have to apologise to you," was how Dora started. "I am wrong and I realise this now."

The two words that Dora had uttered did not make sense to her, because they had never been used ever in all their years as friends. 'Apologise' and 'wrong,' they were so foreign that Fanny doubted herself and that her hearing was actually working anymore. She had started to panic and was having an anxiety attack, she was probably having a heart attack and even worse maybe she was leaving her body. She could only see things around her. *Adieu, cruel world.*

Dora looked at her and with a pained expression said, "I did exactly what I said we mustn't: walk along a street because the guide book said so. I didn't think of where to go, so therefore I made us walk and walk. My word, I am so sorry. In hindsight, when I look at it, yes, we saw some shops and some buildings, but I missed the experience of being able to stop, look and enjoy. My word, Fanny, and to think you warned me this morning of this and I didn't listen."

Fanny was lost for words; even her mouth had deserted her at this time and she found herself gasping for air like a goldfish.

"From this moment, I want us to look and enjoy. Right, then."

Fanny started to get up because even though she didn't admit it, when those words rang out, it meant they had to go. Dora, did not get up, she remained steadfast in her seat.

Fanny gingerly placed herself back into the chair.

"Finish your water, dear, and then we can go."

The next hour they wandered around the museum looking at art pieces and actually spoke to each other. At one point Dora looked at a mess on a canvas and said, "My word, one can call anything art nowadays, including the paper you rest your paint brush on!"

"Fair point Dora," Fanny responded, "I quite like that."

"There you are," Dora exclaimed, "and that is what matters, someone has to look at it and enjoy it. What a wonderful lesson I have been taught today."

Fanny wished she had a recorder because it sounded like Dora was finally losing it and she would need to document the decline.

"Are you ready for the next spot? I do know why I want to visit Liberdade. It has the largest population of Japanese people outside of Japan and in South America. I thought it would be interesting to see it and have lunch there."

"Then let's go forth in pursuit of our next adventure," said a voice which emanated from none other than her own lips.

❈ ❈ ❈

They were both shrieking with laughter like two little schoolgirls who had just been introduced to a sugar high. In each of their hands they had two sticks and with these sticks they were attempting to do some very strange things.

"I can't!" Dora exclaimed, as the two sticks fell onto the table and the man in front of them raised his eyebrow in concern.

"Well, I think I am kind of getting the hang of this." Fanny had managed to grasp the piece of ginger on her plate but as quickly as she gripped it, she had to let it go again.

More laughter. This time the very kind waiter sat at the table with them and said, "I have knife ... fork."

"No, I am not giving up," Dora responded. "I will use chopsticks or I will not eat, it is as simple as that. I would never have thought in a million years that I would be eating sushi in Sao Paulo in South America. After all Fanny, I had to persuade you to eat raw fish and you thought I was mad, so maybe you are not wanting to use them on purpose!"

"Ooh, if I knew it was that easy to get out of trying it I would have definitely tried harder not to make it work, but as you can see, I managed to pick up a piece of ginger," Fanny said with a wicked smile, which had replaced the diplomatic one which was normally plastered on her face.

The man smiled and with a gentle kindness asked them to follow him as he demonstrated once more how to use the two sticks. They raised their chopsticks like he did and he carefully showed them how to open and close them. They repeated, but not before Dora flicked the one chopstick over the table and into the soy sauce below. It splashed dangerously close to her. She tried again and this time was able to get it right. Once they looked like they had mastered this, they then attempted to pick up the pieces of sushi. Fanny was able to balance the food and Dora attempted to cheat and peg the food with the chopstick into her mouth, but she didn't want to get caught.

They both wagged their fingers at her and she put her hands up as if they were holding a gun at her. After a fourth attempt, Dora finally got it and so then the waiter mimed taking the food to their mouths. Although it looked somewhat painful they both managed to do it, and when they deposited the food into their mouths, the waiter clapped in delight and so did they, after dropping their chopsticks onto the table.

The rest of the meal was filled with similar moments, but by the end of it they had learned to use chopsticks and had managed to eat a full meal.

"Well done Fanny," Dora said as if she had actually done the teaching and Fanny was her pupil.

"It was fun, wasn't it?" Fanny replied.

"I would never have thought that I would learn to use chopsticks in Brazil, not Asia." Dora mused.

"Yes, it is rather strange. And I never thought I would ever eat raw fish!"

"Well good for you, you did something that you can tell other people about for the rest of your life. I remember the first time John's special friend -- what's his name? I must stop referring to him as his 'Asian friend,' It's…it's… Jong, that's right, it's Jong and he is from…um…Korea. They also have a kind of sushi, *kimbap*, there and Jong made me some to taste, but I ate it with a fork. I didn't think I could, but it was something that I had to just think differently about, and this trip is about doing things differently. I am going to try to do things differently. This was outright fun. It was the most fun that I have had today. In fact this episode has been the most fun I have had all year. I really need to learn to let go," Dora proclaimed.

"I guess we all do," Fanny considered.

"To fun!" Dora raised her water glass as if this was the finest champagne in the world.

"To fun," Fanny responded, "Ching, ching!"

Even the waiter was beaming at them when they left, clearly he had also enjoyed the experience. They paid for their lunch and went back to walking around the streets, which were not like the Avenida Paulista - all ordered and perfect – these streets were the home of immigrants and were vibrant in colour and full sense of strange writing, which looked like the squiggles they had seen in the Museu de Arte de São Paulo. This is where everything merged together and this is where they could appreciate Sao Paulo, the city of contrasts.

Chapter Eight
Brazil
-Paraty

"P-A-A-R-A-A-T-E-E-E" she exclaimed, looking at Dora for backup.

"That is better, it sounds more like what it should sound like," the man at the bus ticket office said. "How many tickets?"

"Two, please." Fanny quickly replied.

Dora had purposefully decided that it was best to let Fanny be more of a part of the holiday experience and had suggested she purchase the bus tickets to their next destination. This had not been what Fanny wanted though! She quite liked not having to stress and interact with the world beyond. Then, as if to prove the point that she should not, she had not pronounced the name of the town correctly, and it was only when she showed him the name on one of Dora's printouts that the man had corrected her and made her say the correct version, or as close as she could get to it.

With the two tickets, they negotiated the bags onto the bus and settled down for the six-hour journey from Sao Paulo to Paraty. Dora, who had relinquished her rights to the trip for a few minutes, was happy to be back in control and in no time was filling Fanny in on the ins and outs of this little seaside town.

"In the historic past, the town was en route from Sao Paulo to Rio de Janeiro but then came the more exciting highway connection and the city was lost in time, literally. There is an historic town centre which is pretty much as it was, with cobbled streets and old classic buildings." With this she looked up and, quick to correct any perceptions created, added, "We are, however, staying at a little guesthouse just outside of the historic town, next to the ocean."

"How lovely," Fanny responded, and with that there was no more discussion, but as Fanny was sitting by the window she watched as the city of Sao Paulo disappeared and the open road gave way to more scenic views. She was in a bus in the middle of Brazil -- she was going to say this a lot -- but she had not thought this would ever have been possible and not at her age.

When they arrived in Paraty, they were met by the guesthouse owner whom Dora had corresponded with. In no time they were unpacked and looking over the lovely sea in front of them.

"We are going to live dangerously, Fanny," Dora chuckled, "we are going to walk along this beach and have dinner from one of those makeshift restaurants."

"But, um…" Fanny reached desperately for the words, "what about food safety?"

"Well Fanny, look at it like this: if things go horribly wrong, and they may, it's a good cleanse of all that's inside!" Dora thought this was so funny that she was laughing as she was saying it.

"Right then," Fanny said, and then looked even more alarmed, because she was using Dora's words now too.

The walk along the beach was beautiful and the sand was soft. Along the walkway were many makeshift restaurants that consisted of the most basic plastic chairs, and crude structures made out of wood.

Dora carefully looked them over and then proclaimed with her index finger, "That one, I think that is our best bet."

"Why do you say that?" Fanny asked, not sure that the most run-down option was even an option to begin with.

"Well, look how busy it is, there are people standing in a queue. It must be good or else they wouldn't have customers."

Dora, the old Dora, marched up to the rickety structure, and with that, they joined the queue.

They did not have to wait for long before a table became available, but not before they were looked at, pointed at and in one case even given a toddler, because the toddler was screaming at the parents and even more so when the ladies approached them. Dora was at fault in this case, as she had waved at the little one and he had waved back.

Without any English, they were shown what was on offer: grilled fish and a salad-looking accompaniment. They were also shown the soft drinks in the cooler box, and that is how they ordered their meal in Paraty.

"Dora," Fanny said, "This is delicious," chomping on her fish. She even smiled.

"That it is," Dora responded.

"Well, looks like another one of those heavenly experiences," Fanny exclaimed while looking over the beach at the bright orange setting sun and the clouds framed above it.

"This is where we need a Ricky Martin song," Dora laughed, "and we could dance the night away."

"Ricky Martin's not Brazilian, is he?" were the words that floated into the night.

❀ ❀ ❀

They were standing outside each of their respective doors and Dora said, "Right then, so if you feel like the earth is going to move or to put it more impolitely, if the 'runs' come, you are going to knock on my door three times like this." With that she rapped on her door as if the occupant inside was deaf and would feel the vibrations of the exercise to come to the door.

Doors along the corridor started to open as the occupants of the rooms thought someone was at their very door.

Fanny looked awkwardly at them and then the smile came, and the words, "So sorry about the knock, it was an accident." It wasn't an accident, nor was she the one who had actually knocked, but she couldn't help it if 'that' person swung into sequence. Would she have managed the problem in any other way?

The doors closed and Dora, who had remained silent throughout the ordeal, simply carried on, "I have the stomach pills in my medical kit and we will have you back in business in no time."

"I didn't know you had a medical kit," Fanny said.

"Yes, one never knows when I might need to operate on you, here in the wild jungles of Brazil." Guffaw, guffaw…snigger…snigger. With that she opened her door and disappeared, leaving Fanny in the hallway.

Fanny once again questioned her sanity. She had witnessed Dora make a joke, and not only make the joke but laugh at the joke at the same time. This was unheard of. No one would believe her if she were to tell them.

It was, however, not the joke that was disturbing her the most at this time. This was not something one spoke about, one did not really discuss the delicate issues of illness associated with…well, you know…well she just couldn't think about it, let alone talk about it. For now her stomach was holding up and there were no signs of any undue problems on the horizon, but if…oh dear…what if…

❀ ❀ ❀

The next morning over breakfast Dora asked, "Sleep well?"

"Yes, thank you, I did" Fanny responded casually.

Dora continued to look at her as if waiting for more. She smiled back and Dora continued to stare. "So did you have 'the runs'?" This was rather loudly announced.

Fanny wanted to crawl under the table in shame, and, biting her cheek and putting on the diplomatic face all at once, said under her breath, "No, the constitution is sound, thank you."

"There you are," Dora continued, "what did I tell you? You would be fine! Right then…"

❀ ❀ ❀

"Bloody hell," it just came out, "these cobbled streets could be used as a weapon of mass destruction."

Dora did not hear her, or at least pretended not to.

The old town was picturesque and the streets, true to their description, were indeed cobbled, but Fanny was trying to balance and make sure she did not trip as she made her way along.

The shops on either side of the street were filled with local goods and they both enjoyed being able to look at the local art and culture. It was fun to meander down from one side to the next.

Later in the morning, they bought some cold drinks and sat in Matriz Square enjoying the experience.

"I have an idea," Dora said, "it goes back to what we discussed about places to visit. In this case, we didn't have to see a specific building; rather we had an experience of wondering through an historic town. The very act of simply looking is what makes it fun. There is something I want to try though, but it's not the season."

"And what would that be?"

"A mudslinging contest."

"Dora, I apologise, but my hearing is not what it used to be. For a moment there I thought you said you wanted to go on a mudslinging contest. Sorry, dear, could you repeat what you said?"

"Well, that is exactly what I said," Dora confirmed.

Fanny started to choke on the last of the liquid that was about to make its way down her throat. It was so bad that Dora had to intervene and do a hybrid of the Heimlich manoeuvre.

"It happens here in Paraty, that you wade around in the mud for a few hours, dance a bit here, jog a bit over there and then you parade through the streets showing off your browner body!"

Fanny lifted her hand up and rather comically indicated, "Hell, no!"

Dora smiled back at her and then laughed, "It will be fun!"

"This is not learning to use chopsticks, this is wading around in a mess! And considering the size of me, they might mistake me for a hippopotamus and

I might be roasted on an open fire somewhere along there in the makeshift restaurants on the beach. No, thank you very much!"

Dora did not seem offended by her decision, and quietly sat back and continued to smile while staring out at the square in front of her.

Chapter Nine

Brazil
-Rio De Janeiro

Fanny opened the curtains and looked outside at the sun-filled street. This city was strangely quiet this time of day. It was still very early and as Dora and she had agreed to breakfast only an hour later, she decided to head down to the famous Copacabana beach to look at the ocean and have some time to absorb this new space.

She quickly dressed and headed out of the lobby and into the streets. Within minutes she found herself looking at the white expanse of sand in front of her and she could not help smiling. She was in Rio de Janeiro and like before, when she had thought very little of the trip, she found that waking up each morning to a new adventure and opportunity to explore a city and country was infectious.

The beach was really wide and she took her sandals off and felt the squishy sand between her toes. She walked towards the water and considered that in front of her was an expanse that could not be further from the United Kingdom, this water that flowed and crashed and mixed and laughed with the beautiful people of Brazil.

The water was cool and washed around her feet. She looked now into the waves in front of her to notice that some people were swimming in the early morning. Simply delightful, she felt. As she looked further to her right, she noticed something that was really white, almost shimmering in its purity, bobbing around in the water. It must be one of those buoys that are used as markers to indicate swimming areas, she thought, and was about to turn around and return to the beach when she noticed that the buoy was moving. *Her eyes*, she thought; it was time to come to terms with the fact that she no longer was able to see as well as she had hoped.

When she looked again, the white object, which was so white that it reflected the light with a force, was now moving directly to her. She became alarmed; maybe this was a secret observation machine and was going to kidnap her and sell her to a drug lord for a small fee. She started backing out of the water, never taking her eyes off of the approaching craft.

She was out of the water and once more on the safety of the beach. She watched in morbid fascination as the craft came all the way to the where the waves were breaking onto the sand. It was only then that she saw that this was not a craft, not some conspiracy theorist's vehicle, but none other than Dora, in a swimming costume, who broke through the surface of the water wearing goggles and smiling brightly. That white beacon was her very pale, white legs which were in the water.

"Cooee, cooee over there! Morning Fanny, fancy a dip?" she said, while treading water in front of her.

"My word, Dora, you scared the daylights out of me," Fanny exclaimed.

"Didn't think you were up, or I would have invited you to join me in my morning swim."

Fanny had to bite her tongue not to share what she had thought Dora was. It was not the fact that she had imagined she was a foreign object, it was the fact that, compared to all of the other people swimming in the sea, her very, very, very white skin had stood out and seemed unnatural, almost foreign, almost non-human.

Dora had now stood up and was next to her wrapping her towel around herself. The sea was in front of them, Sugar Loaf mountain was behind them and they stood staring and not saying a thing for a few minutes. Dora then threw on her t-shirt and shorts and with that, the look returned, that look. "Right then," Dora said, "it's time for breakfast."

With that indirect command, they found themselves walking -- not marching, Fanny thought -- across the beach and back towards the hotel. Maybe some things were changing.

❦ ❦ ❦

It was over breakfast that Dora outlined the plans for the day, they were going to go on a day tour of the city, visiting the statue of Christ the Redeemer, the famous one on top of that mountain which welcomed the world. Then they were going up Sugar Loaf Mountain on the cable car, and afterwards they were going for a general drive through the city, before returning to the lovely Copacabana. Dora looked up, actually for the first time ever, and asked, "Does this sound good?"

Whereas before Fanny would have felt the panic of travel knotting up her stomach and killing her appetite (no, that was not correct; stimulating her appetite for more food), she now looked forward to these morning strategy sessions in which the plans of the day were discussed.

"Sounds delightful, Dora, thank you," Fanny said, "excited that we are going with a tour company around the city…" She realised too late that she might have offended Dora. "That is not what I meant, Dora, I truly appreciate your guiding us…"

"No offence taken, Fanny. When we can go on a tour I like the idea of experts telling us about their town or city. Sometimes, though, these have not gotten good reviews, or do not exist, hence I have done them myself."

The ride through the streets left her buzzing as she saw a different side of Brazil. These were not the streets of Sao Paulo with their sophistication and chic; this was rawer actually. Soon she saw a scrambling of shanty houses which dotted the side of the hill. She was confused as she turned to Dora and asked, "What are those buildings?"

"*Favelas*. They are low-cost housing no, sorry, that is not fair. They were built by the poorer members of the city to live in because they could not afford something better." Dora said.

"But Dora, some look really makeshift." Fanny responded concerned.

"Well, they are."

"They must be a health and safety risk?" Fanny said.

"More than that, they are also filled with crime, mostly poverty-related, and are dangerous places to survive in."

"I didn't know," Fanny's brow was furrowed at what she had seen and what she was hearing.

"There are tours that you can go on and visit them."

"Is it safe?" Fanny responded with panic in her voice.

"I didn't look at it in that way. I didn't want to visit because I was worried we would be looking at poorer people as if we were going to a zoo," Dora said cautiously.

"Whatever do you mean?"

"Well, there is a whole debate online between the two sides; those that see visiting and coming to terms with this kind of reality as healthy because you learn about how people live. The other side feel that you are treating the experience like an attraction – you are looking and pointing and in effect treating the people as the attraction."

"My word," Fanny exclaimed.

Dora looked pensive and then said, "I don't know what to think anymore, but I didn't want to participate in anything that had any concerns linked to it. There was a whole section on responsible tourism and I joined a group that promotes responsible tourism in the world and each country has its own chapter."

"That is very honourable of you Dora,"

"That is very kind," Dora responded, "but I want our footprint on this trip to be linked to things that encourage local economic empowerment and which ensure that the environment and the rights of people are considered."

This all sounded very complicated and Fanny felt the smile return to her lips and looked at Dora with a somewhat confused face.

"You don't have to do the same as me. I would like you to see my point of view, but will respect your decision."

Fanny looked admirably at Dora, "I understand now; you have spent lots of time reading up about the various sites and some have some controversy linked to it and you are worried that should we visit we may contribute to further problems?"

"Exactly," Dora replied.

"I have the greatest respect for you, so whatever you have decided must be the better solution."

With that they went into a quiet time, in which the sounds of the bus they were on hummed along. The streets whisked by and they were once more looking at the Corcovado rising in front of them with that ever-famous statue on it.

They were dropped at the funicular stop and climbed inside, waiting to be transported to the top. It felt like a roller coaster ride up the mountain. Fanny held onto the seat in front of her despite the fact that there was someone sitting there, irritated with her for digging her fingers into his back each time the funicular made a turn or hung at an obscure angle as it made its way up.

It took a full two minutes for Dora to break the clasp that Fanny had on the seat in front of her once they had reached the top of the mountain. It took another minute to drag her out of the funicular and another minute for her to respond to light and other stimuli, while standing on the exit platform.

"Bloody hell!" It was Dora this time who made the statement and Fanny continued to blink and stare at her.

"Tell me we are going to drive down?" Fanny begged.

"No, nothing that boring," Dora chortled, "nothing wrong with a bit of fun, eh!"

"Hmmm," is all Fanny could muster as Dora lead them towards the escalators that would take them up to the statue.

Christ the Redeemer soared above them and they were dwarfed by the sheer magnitude of the statue. Fanny just looked up and stared in awe. What did it take to create a work like this, the time thinking about the look and then the painstaking time it would take to manufacture it? "It's even more spectacular than I ever thought it would be."

Dora was equally struck by it and replied, "That it is."

"Let's go to the vantage point over there," Dora motioned, where people were gathered to take pictures of the statue behind them.

She couldn't understand why all these people were hunched together and then taking out these little black squares and smiling. In fact no one had cameras at all, which Fanny thought was unusual. Didn't people want a memory of their trip abroad? She took out her camera and took a few photographs and took an interesting shot of Dora looking towards the statue with her face half turned and then another one when she looked towards her, but not in a pose but a completely natural way. Fanny could feel she was taking some real gems up here.

She turned to the two tourists on her left and asked, "Would you take a picture of my friend and I?"

They didn't speak English but understood what she was asking. She huddled close to Dora and the two of them beamed with joy on top of that mountain.

When she collected her camera from the two, she motioned that she would take a picture of them with theirs. They just looked at her strangely and she smiled and walked away quickly. "I don't know what it is with these people on this mountain. but no one but us are taking pictures!"

"Yes, they are Fanny, look everyone is."

She looked again but could not see it, where were the cameras? "Who?"

Fanny pointed out the little black boxes that were in almost every hand, "The cameras are all in their phones. They are all taking 'selfies'."

"Self-what?" Fanny asked, confused.

"'Selfies', it's what the young use as a phrase to indicate a photo without the help of others, basically one in which you take the photo yourself."

"Whatever do you mean?"

"Well John and Jong take them all the time," Dora explained, "they have a camera built into their phone and the camera has a lens in the front as well as the back of the phone, so they can take a photo themselves without the need to ask others to take it."

"Don't be silly Dora," Fanny laughed, "I am not going to fall for that one."

Dora marched over to a group of students engrossed in playing with their hands and mimicking the statue's hands. "F-AAAA-NNNNNNN-YYYYY!" she roared.

Fanny came running and saw that true to her word, there was a picture on the screen of one of those black boxes of the student with the scrawny look and the statue in the background. She was fascinated. By holding the black box ahead, they could capture themselves into the picture. Now she was convinced that she was having an out-of-body experience and that her frame of reality had been kidnapped by another being. This did not make any logical sense to her; it was so foreign, how was this even possible? She desperately wanted to utter the words that had come to define her on this trip, but seeing that she was so close to the statue and that in fact, He was watching, made her bite her tongue to refrain from uttering something blasphemous. "I want to take a selfish," she said to Dora.

"A 'selfie', it's called a 'selfie'!"

❀ ❀ ❀

It was indeed a day of heights and mountains, Fanny found herself precariously dangling from a cable car between the two parts of Sugar Loaf Mountain, wondering if she was insured, in the event of one of the cables breaking. Not that there would be any evidence, because they did not have a telephone with one of those camera thingies to take the 'selfish', so there would be no evidence of them ever having been to Sugar Loaf Mountain, oh dear!

"Breathe, Fanny, breathe," Dora chimed from the side of the car where she was looking in earnest at the view below. Then, with a wicked smile; yes, the most wicked to date, Dora said, "And if all else fails, look up and think of England!" Chortle, chortle, chortle.

This was not funny!

When they reached the first peak, Dora left the car in a hurry to see what lay below. Fanny hurried after her. There was the whole of the city below, from the beaches of the Copacabana, to the city in between. How lucky they were to be able to see this beauty, Fanny thought, as the horror of the cable car ride disappeared and was replaced with this wonder.

"Dora!" She ran after her to make sure that she heard what was coming next. "Dora, I have to say this right now. We are going to get one of those phone thingies and we are going to take a 'shellfish' at every place we visit. We are then going to put them all together, because I want a memory of you and me in all of these spectacular places. It may be too late for the places that we have already been to -- we will have those as normal photographs -- but I insist that we get one, please, I am begging you, we need to get a 'selfish'."

Dora gave her that look, and then said, "Now, unless you say it correctly, I am not going to listen anymore. It is not 'selfish' and certainly not 'shellfish'; it is a 'selfie', 'fie'. Say after me three times, 'selfie', 'selfie', 'selfie'."

Fanny beamed and with a concentration that would have made Gary Kasparov look like a Disney character, she said with sincere determination, "'Selfie'... 'selfie'... 'selfie'!"

"Right then," Dora said, and Fanny knew they were going to get that damn thingy as soon as they were on their own.

Fanny couldn't think of another thing on the second cable car ride other than getting the thingy, and so the fear that had enveloped her on the first ride was completely gone. This was despite the fact that the second move to the higher peak was far wilder, the ride infinitely scarier.

The second peak was even more spectacular and she was now buzzing about in delight and noticing all the people that were taking photos on their own. What she had thought was ridiculous now made perfect sense. That was going to be her in a few hours. What a shame they would not have photographs up to this point. There was no time like the present.

When they reached the base of the mountain where their tour bus was waiting for them, Fanny rushed to the tour leader and asked, "Where can I get one of those thingies that takes the 'selfies'?"

The man looked at her confused. "I am sorry Madam, not understand."

She would need Dora, "D-OOOOO-RRRR-AAAA!"

Dora looked over at the two of them with a certain suspicion. "I want to know where we can get a selfie machine. Can you try and explain it to him?"

"Right then," Dora took control, "where in Rio de Janeiro can we buy one of those phones with a camera in it?"

He seemed to understand this concept and as the morning tour was coming to an end he said, "If you want instead of drop you at hotel, I drop you electronic shop?"

Fanny clapped her hands in delight. "I am getting a 'selfie' machine; I am getting a 'selfie' machine!" Dora looked like she was excited about the latest course of events too.

In no time they were sitting in a large electronic shop with a man who spoke passionately with his hands, showing them the range of phones available. He was eager to show the phone functions and the fact that it could play music and do a multitude of other things. "I want to see the 'selfie' thing," she said, not interested in the rest. With that, he prepared the thingy to do it and there was a very close-up picture of Fanny's face in mid-sentence, one of her from a more respectable distance and then two with her and Dora, and even one where they had hauled the salesman into the shot. The look of sheer terror on his face was perfect!

Dora looked at Fanny and said, "Never in my life would I ever think you would get a phone, a cellular phone. Fanny is buying a cellular phone."

"Not just any phone," the man said, "it is a 'smartphone'."

Fanny looked at both of them and smiled, "smartie phone, or cell thingy for me it will always be the 'selfie' maker." And with that she stroked it as if it was a small animal in her arms for the first time.

And there, at that age -- well, it is not important to know the exact age as that would be rude to ask, but at a later time in her life -- Fanny was not only living life but was also the brand new owner of a 'selfie' maker. "Now teach me from scratch once more. Dora, are you watching?" In the shop alone there

49

must have been over a hundred photographs, but as the man explained they would not be printed unless she wanted them. This was simply fascinating. So she could take photographs to her heart's content and all would be stored in the machine and she could then choose what to print.

It was then that a further idea came to her, she was going to put together a photo journal which she would intersperse with the entrance tickets, or restaurant bills or whatever else she managed to pick up. This was going to be her joy over the next months. It would also allow her to keep her memories alive.

She was given the charger, the paperwork, the explanation for the phone, the box and even a hug from the salesman. Now if only she had gotten a 'selfie' of that because he was rather delightful, she had decided, with a silent grin to herself. Hmmm, life was looking good indeed.

❁ ❁ ❁

The next morning Fanny made a point of waking up early and accompanying Dora on her morning swim. While Dora frolicked in the waves, she took pictures of the beach, of people on the beach and most importantly, of herself against the backdrop of the beach, the mountain and the sea.

Dora had given her some sound advice. "Careful when you use the device and make sure that you do not let it out of your sight." Fanny was very careful to place the phone in the cover that she had been given by the shop as a gift.

Even breakfast was captured as part of the morning shooting spree. With no worries about costly printouts she took a photograph of pretty much anything that moved. Dora at one point had to manually push the phone out of her face as she was trying to place a carefully planned forkful of food into her mouth.

"Down, put the device down, now!" Dora commanded.

Fanny responded automatically and the phone was placed on the table. To make her point, Dora said, "Stay!"

Fanny nodded obediently.

"Well today is one of those days when I am going to have to ask, if you would like to come with me or would prefer to spend some time on your own?"

"Whatever do you mean?" Fanny asked.

"Well, let's just say I am being quite self-obsessed today as I want to go somewhere to which I could only dream of going, but it might not be to your liking."

"Well tell me and let me decide," Fanny said.

"Right then, I will just come out with it." However, there was nothing after this statement. To make the point, Fanny rather dramatically went to pick up the phone, which got the required attention and right reaction.

"All right," Dora said and motioned with her finger to Fanny's hands which were reaching for the phone, "I want to go to the Carmen Miranda Museum. There; I said it." Dora did not make eye contact, but rather, looked down at the tablecloth.

"Who is that?" Fanny asked confused.

"Carmen Miranda?" Dora gasped. "Only the most amazing star of the screen, who could use platform shoes to tower above the mountains we saw yesterday, and whose head pieces were legendary. Who else could wear a fruit basket packed with fruit on their head and look as glamorous as could be?" When Dora said this she mimed the head piece on her head and even articulated the pieces of fruit jutting out with round movements of her hands.

"I see," Fanny said still unsure of what to say.

"If you don't want to go I will completely understand, but I beg that you let me go and see the costumes in person."

"Dora," Fanny smiled mischievously, "think of how many 'selfies' we can take," and with that it was decided.

❈ ❈ ❈

51

Dora had warned Fanny that the museum was hard to find, was going to be quite a ride, literally in a taxi, and would require some patience. Fanny smiled in response to this, but these explanations were upsetting her less and less and the two found themselves in the back of a taxi winding through the streets of Rio de Janeiro. After many twists, turns and indeed a quick drive up a one way street in the wrong direction, they found themselves outside the sign for the Carmen Miranda Museum.

This was the first stop for the 'selfie' of the two of them looking focused towards the camera with the sign in the background. If yesterday had been a day of excitements for Fanny, today was a day of absolute excitement for Dora. She could not contain herself and was shaking when she paid for the tickets.

Dora hurried inside the museum doors, as if all the sweets in Ireland had been sanctioned and had been given away only to her. Inside, it was a marvel to observe in a small area the films playing Carmen Miranda. But it was what was on display in front of them that could only be described as out-of-this-world!

Fanny looked on as Dora walked like a somnambulist towards a display case -- not just any display case, but one which held in its ambit the greatest sight in the world. In front of them were the largest, highest platform shoes she had ever seen. "Goodness me," was what Dora said. Fanny managed to take photographs of Dora just staring, her mouth half-open and her eyes glued to what she saw. It was like Dora could not move.

"Dora, I never knew you were a fan?" Fanny said.

"I have been obsessed with her all my life."

She came back to life and muttered words like, "Awesome, "Beautiful," "Misanthropic," throughout the movement between the different displays.

Like the movement at the sight of the shoes, she was once again sucked into the vortex and Dora looked in awe at a display with a head piece with absolutely everything but the kitchen sink on it. Fanny could not resist and out came the device ready to capture the moment forever on film -- sherbet, there wasn't any film -- well, capture it electronically! Dora stood for over five minutes just staring, and then finally said, "She just lived life as someone who was petite, but she made sure to live larger than life at all times. She expressed herself in colour, extravagance and *joie de vivre*."

"You can say that again," Fanny said snapping a selfie with her and the headpiece.

"It is so sad that she died a victim of narcotics and booze," Dora sighed when she said this, "don't they all."

"Well look at it like this, these were her chopsticks, or her smartphones, or whatever else brings you joy. And she must have enjoyed life to have been able to express herself like this."

"Thank you for saying that," Dora agreed.

"Come on, this is 'selfie' heaven," and with that they took photograph after photograph.

Even after they had been through all the displays Dora said, "I have to do it again; please, I will be quick."

Fanny didn't mind and sat down to watch the clips of Carmen Miranda on screen. Priceless! She was so enthralled by what she was watching that only much later did she notice Dora sitting next to her staring ahead. Then, she quietly took out her little selfie device and captured the most beautiful shot of Dora, one that Dora didn't even notice was being taken.

When the film came to the end of the loop, Dora was clasping her hands and smiling broadly.

"Could we go to one more place?" Dora asked carefully.

"I am up for visiting a hundred more places," Fanny bubbled.

"Well it is to go to the Jardim Botanico, the botanical gardens. I would like my last memory of this beautiful city to be of the beauty of nature which is what it has so much of."

"Right then," Fanny stood back as she said this -- was this not the second time that she had become Dora?

They bundled into another taxi and were once again flying through the streets giggling like two teenagers on a cheap high of sugar carbonated drinks.

They spent the remainder of the morning wandering around the different gardens, looking at the abundance of flowers and plants.

Dora knew so much about flowers and could recite the names of the various plants and even explain their origins. Fanny was delighted and clicked away -- well not clicked, tapped away -- taking pictures galore.

Then by chance they came upon the Japanese section of the gardens and were once again transported to the chopstick incident in Sao Paulo. "Well, we are constantly reminded of differences, aren't we?" Dora considered.

"That we are, but how absolutely tranquil," Fanny replied.

The different spaces and the symmetry all in such contrast to the other wilder parts of the gardens.

In the middle of the garden was a tea shop and on offer was none other than green tea, and, well, there you have it.

Chapter 10
Brazil
-Foz do Iguaçu

"There are supposed to be hundreds of varieties of birds within the bird park," Dora explained to Fanny. Their visit to Foz do Iguaçu had been for the purposes of seeing the Iguaçu Falls but en route was this bird park and they had decided to go inside and take a look.

"That is a lot," Fanny said.

"I don't know how I feel about animals in captivity," Dora said with much thought.

"Well, at least there are open aviaries here and we can see the birds have some movement," Fanny noted.

"Yes," Dora replied, "it is just that it feels enclosed, worrying about them not being able to be completely free. It's another one of those dilemmas that I have been thinking a lot about."

"If one considers how much damage there is to the environment, these kinds of initiatives could possibly help."

"You make a good point..." Dora pondered.

Fanny looked at Dora again in surprise: she had mentioned that Fanny made sense. My word!

"I am also a hypocrite because I want the animals to be free, and yet I am quite happy to eat them. In fact, I could never be vegetarian because I like a bird too much. Chicken, it's my absolute weakness as you know."

Fanny laughed, "I certainly can't give up my roast chicken on a Sunday!"

And with that they were moving through the aviaries looking at the colourful birds in front of them and happily taking 'selfies' where they could.

It was when they got to the section where butterflies could be seen that

Dora said, "I now know why the caged bird sings." This went completely over Fanny's head.

"Why would that be?"

"It's an expression, Fanny; don't you remember Oprah and her friend that writer Maya Angelou?"

"No, I can't say I know Maya the bee, but I do know Oprah."

"Maya Angelou! Only one of the greatest writers about the spirit of a human."

"Well then why is she writing about birds?"

"It's a metaphor!"

"Right…" Fanny could see this was going to turn into an English lesson and with her new found independence pointed at the butterflies and said, "Look, butterflies."

It did not work. Dora instead raised her eyebrows and looking at Fanny, said, "We have the ability to soar but we are scared to do so. These birds could have had a life of freedom but they were captured and kept here. Yes, they still have a life and it is at least decent. However, can you imagine them soaring through the Amazon jungle or living on a rooftop in Rio de Janeiro with views of the Copacabana?"

"I think what you are trying to say to me is that we need to be aware that living on a roof could be fun." Fanny smiled at her own joke, although Dora did not.

"No Fanny, I am saying that we should make the most of life while we can. I had only ever travelled to Ireland and I thought I had seen it all. Here I have had more fun in the last ten days than I have had in my entire life, and all because I thought I was content."

Fanny nodded her head and looked at her phone which was in her hand and was pointing at the floor ready to capture the next image.

"I have learnt a great lesson and I am truly thankful," Dora said.

The rest of the time they wandered around but neither spoke.

❈ ❈ ❈

"Bloody hellllll!!!!!!!" Fanny screamed above the roar of the Iguaçu Falls. Dora and her were strapped into a little boat and were being tossed around the currents of the water below the falls. Dora raised her hands at intermittent intervals as if she was on a rollercoaster, mostly because the boat was full of students doing the same. The captain dunked the boat and they were covered in spray yet again.

"F-AAAAA-NNN-YYYYY," Dora yelled, "this is so much fun!"

Fanny, who would not have ever dared to do something like this before, was only worried about capturing as many shots of the falls as she could, and in order to do this she needed to wrap and unwrap her phone in a plastic sleeve she had been given. She raised her thumb up and gave off a smile. It was pointless trying to talk, so sign language it was going to be.

They continued to move about and each turn gave off new wonders, new sprays, until her hair was soaked, even though she had put on the plastic raincoat when she had boarded the boat. The falls were ferocious and alive and never stopped. The water just surged and fell all around them. She thought the falls would be dainty but how wrong she was; they were anything but dainty.

"Photo, take the photo!" the captain shouted, and with that the camera was hastily unwrapped and Fanny took picture after picture of the falls close up. The captain then smiled, indicated they should wrap up and yelled even louder, "Now we go Devil's Throat, hope you got insurance!" His laughs could be heard behind them as they were once more sprayed.

Dora looked like a drowned rat and she knew she felt like one. Fanny did too. She would have to capture this when they got back to land. After all, memories were not only about the things that looked pretty.

The boat continued to show them the different faces of the falls and when they were safely back on land, the roar of the falls was still echoing in their ears.

"Come we are going to take as many 'selfies' as we can of the different sides of the falls," Fanny said grabbing Dora's arm and dragging her to the walkways. The picture of them both looking water soaked and slightly sea-wrecked made them both shriek with laughter. Dora was laughing so much that she grabbed the sides of her stomach as if she was in terrible pain and yet continued to laugh.

They spent the rest of the day walking around and admiring the water, talking, laughing and sharing ideas of new adventures to new destinations.

"We could go and visit all the large waterfalls of the world. I can see a potential for many more trips Fanny, my dear," Dora pronounced.

"That does sound exciting," Fanny replied.

And with that they said goodbye to the Iguaçu Falls and Brazil. As a matter of fact, they were about to board a bus to Buenos Aires, Argentina.

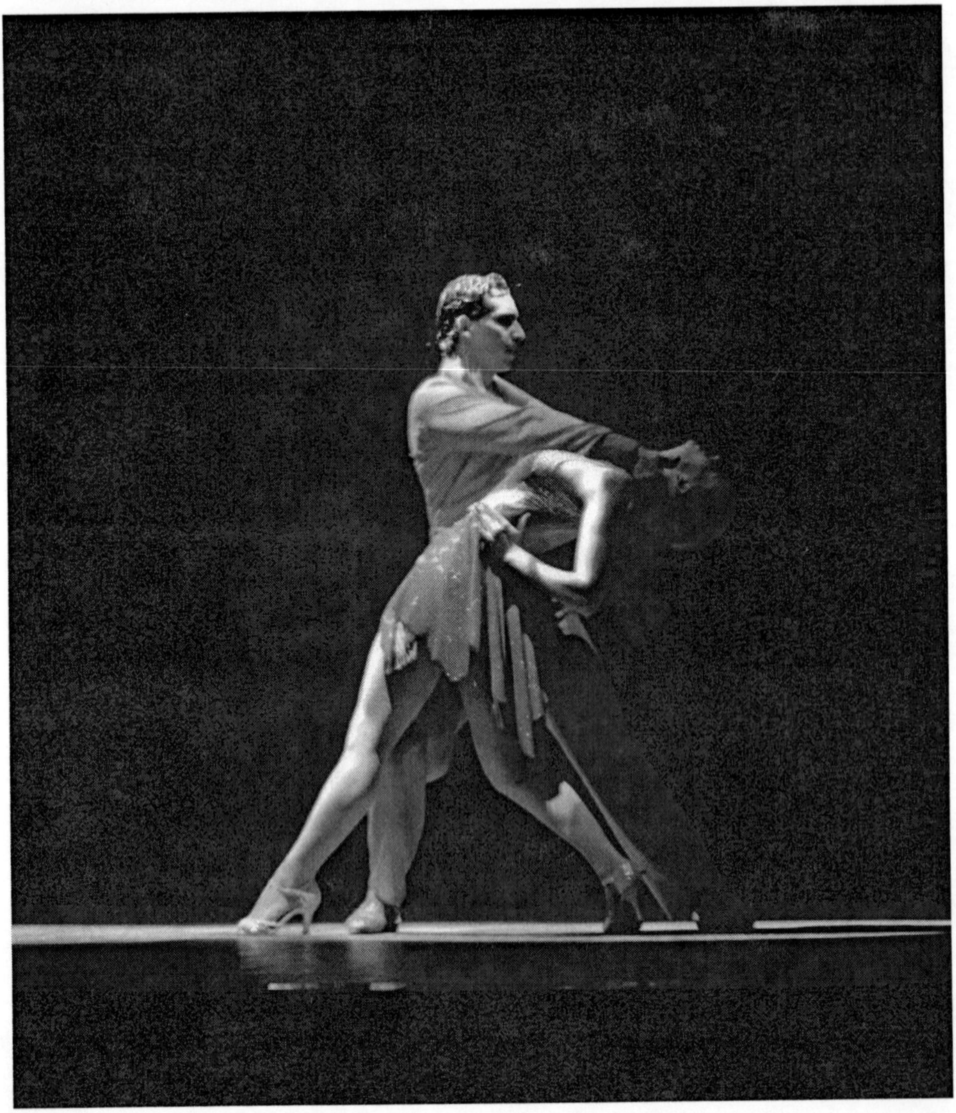

Part Three ~
Cry for me Argentina,
or, simply put:
leave singing to the professionals

Chapter Eleven

Argentina
-Buenos Aires

Fanny could get used to this kind of life. She was sitting in the L'Orangerie restaurant, in the Alvear Palace Hotel in Buenos Aires. This hotel was historic and had tradition, and she was feeling in her element as she looked around at the decor, the furnishings and all the trappings that said this was 'the place' at which to see and be seen. What captured her attention the most was that it was full, and that the waiters and waitresses wore gloves, like people should in a place of this stature.

Who said that elegance and the need to be pampered were not still contained within people? What also made her happy, as she glanced around the room, was that there were not only older people like herself, but families and couples of all ages.

She leaned over to Dora and said, "You do know how to put on a party, old girl," before breaking into a quiet laugh.

"It is lovely, isn't it?" Dora said while sipping gingerly from her tea.

"Now, how did you hear about this place?" Fanny enquired.

"John and Jong told me about it," Dora said. "Trust them to have found this place!"

Fanny smiled and looked at the piano player, who was gently playing a Pachelbel favourite. She was jolted out of her daydream by the arrival of the afternoon treats which made up the tea. This was the real deal, with sandwiches, scones, cakes and other baked treats. Fanny could feel her mouth salivating and she mentally planned what she was going to devour and in what order.

"Excuse me for a second," she heard, as Dora rose and left the table. It didn't have much of an impact on Fanny as she reached for the sandwiches and happily started stuffing her mouth. They were cucumber sandwiches, which meant that they were healthy, right? And she could now eat even more, the delights.

It was then that she heard a terrible sound. Mixed with the sound of the piano was a terrible cacophony which sounded like a cat slowly being murdered with blunt knitting needles. What made it worse was that the tune sounded vaguely familiar.

"D-OOONNNNNNNN-TTTTT CRYYYYYY FOR MEEEE ARGEN-TINNAAAAAAAA," the wailing noise rose above the room and grated on her ears.

"Bloody hell," she said, picking up a little tartlet and popping it into her mouth.

"THE TRUTHHHH IS I NEVVVVERRR LEFFT YOU."

She had to see what was causing this racket and turned around to face the piano. It was then that she had the terrible realisation, one which would come to haunt her for the rest of her life. One which could never, ever, ever be erased. The piano player was being accompanied by a singer, and it was none other than Dora.

It must have been a sugar high, that is all it could have been, she thought, because the reality of the situation was too horrid to contemplate. What made matters decidedly more problematic was that while she had at least carried on eating during the fiasco, most of the tables' inhabitants had simply stopped, and were looking on in shocked horror as Dora held the side of the piano with one hand and looked like one of those creatures from a horror film ready to pounce and kill the innocent victims below.

Should she quietly get up and run out of the restaurant and into the oncoming traffic, or should she pretend she did not know the culprit? She was unable to move and simply stared in horror. It is true what people say about trauma; when you are suffering through it yourself, time does slow down to a deathly, deathly slow speed. To add to this, she simply could not swallow the pastry, and kept on chewing and chewing like a cow with a cud.

When the ordeal did come to an end, there was a smattering of applause and Dora shook the hand of the pianist, whose face was the epitome of pure pain, and walked back to the table.

Everyone was staring and pointing and Dora seemed oblivious to it all. "Well Fanny, it's good to be able to follow your dreams."

Fanny carried on chewing her cud and blinking at Dora, hypnotised by the horror.

"You know, all my life I wanted to perform, I wanted to be able to sing and let others share in my joy of musicals, and I thought, here is an opportunity to do just that. The pianist was ever too kind and even knew 'Don't Cry for Me Argentina' off by heart. What a gem! To be able to sing that song, in this city; knowing that Eva Peron is with me in spirit. Sublime, simply sublime."

If only there could be an earthquake now, Fanny thought. I could be sucked into the depths of the earth and leave this world. But alas, that would not be the case.

"You are lost for words," Dora said, "I am so touched. I never knew my music would have this effect on people. Did you see I had everyone's attention?"

Fanny felt as her mouth forced itself into a smile, but it was painful indeed, as there was still the matter of the undigested food swirling around in her mouth.

"A triumph, a triumph that I did not know I was going to achieve here of all places."

And with that, Dora sat back in her chair, took the phone lying on the table and took a 'selfie' with her and the piano player in the background.

Fanny got that sick feeling: what else was she to expect in this city? They would need to leave as soon as possible!

"Right then," Dora said helping herself to the treats in front of her.

❃ ❃ ❃

Over breakfast Fanny still could not look at Dora. Dora did not detect any problems and was in good spirits and ready for the morning briefing.

"Right then, this is Eva Peron's city. Well then, why not go to the two most iconic venues which celebrate this -- the Casa Rosada, where she lived and the Recoleta, where she continues to live?"

"I thought she was dead," Fanny said.

"It's another figure of speech, Fanny; yes, she is dead and that is why we are going to visit the Recoleta where her body rests."

Fanny was wondering what this could possibly mean? Only time would tell.

They arrived at the Plaza de Mayo, and there was no way to ignore it, there was the iconic building in front of them. "Come, we need to get into the queue for the tour," Dora barked.

"What tour?" Fanny said nervously.

"The tour of the Casa Rosada," Dora said with fervour. "On the weekend you are able to go on a tour of the Casa Rosada and actually see what the Presidents see."

They went through the security scanners repeatedly as Fanny kept beeping. "Bloody hell," she exclaimed, as she was patted down.

Once they had tickets, they lined up in their English-speaking tour group waiting area. The guide who arrived quickly introduced herself and made it clear, "You do not digress from the tour and you stay with me at all times. This is still the working office of the President of Argentina. Any disturbances and you will be arrested. Understand?"

This was all Fanny needed to hear, as she made sure to stand close to the guide at all times during the tour, and not only that, but to stand at attention. The last thing she wanted in her life was to spend her last days in prison. Fanny looked over at Dora and hoped that she understood too.

They wondered through the various rooms taking in hundreds of years of history, the beautiful internal courtyards, and the various state and reception rooms.

They arrived at the office of the President and the guide was quick to point out, "And here is the working office of the President."

Dora and Fanny squashed close together to take a 'selfie'.

"No photographs here," the guide said. Like lightning Fanny returned her phone to her bag, raised her hands up as if she was about to be shot by a water pistol, and made sure to show the guide that she intended to comply under all circumstances.

The guide continued, "This is where Eva Peron sat prior to that iconic speech."

Dora gasped. Fanny edged closer to the guide.

"And now, follow me," the guide said. Fanny made sure she could walk directly next to her.

Then they walked through the doors and were on the balcony of the Casa Rosada where Eva Peron had once stood. This is It. *Don't cry for me, Argentina.* Is that what the guide just said, Fanny thought? No, not really. This is IT. Fanny looked left and right. No, not really either! The guide had simply said, "Take a photo here if you want."

Fanny eyed Dora suspiciously but Dora was simply looking at the Plaza de Mayo in front of her. The 'selfie' would be iconic, the two ladies on the pink balcony. It was when Fanny looked at the other tourists that she realised that the two of them were mild in comparison, because there were people raising their hands as if they were Evita, taking photographs and pulling faces, and one person even yelled at the top of their lungs, "Don't cry for me….."

"Please sir," the guide interrupted, "that is not necessary."

Fanny smiled and felt for the first time that she could forgive Dora for the previous day. After all, it had not been that bad…. Who was she kidding? Yes it had, but people all needed to express themselves in their own unique ways.

At the end of the tour, they went to the museum at the back of the building and were able to see some more of the mementos of various presidents that had held office.

"Time for a coffee," Dora said and they made their way out and into a café nearby.

"Isn't it interesting how coffee has been served differently in every city we have visited?"

"I haven't noticed," Fanny said.

However, when the coffee arrived there was a glass of water and a chocolate accompanying it.

"I think this tells us that every place is unique, even in the ways they do something that each city in the world might do, offer a cup of tea or coffee," Dora summarised.

"Well, I like it," Fanny said, enjoying the chocolate and the strong coffee.

Dora continued, "Think about how politics shape a country."

Here we go, Fanny thought, "Yes…"

"Well, we were in the place where an iconic speech was made," Dora pondered. "If I am not mistaken, I read somewhere that it was also on this balcony that the Falklands War was started. See the contrasts? And here we are, so many years later, as guests of the country going on a tour, but remember that time in the United Kingdom and the bad energy the war created."

"And travel helps to break through the politics and put you in touch with the people and the culture," Fanny added.

"Yes. I have also decided though, I will not visit a country that holds people against their will, like Myanmar held Aan Sang Suu Kyi or like South Africa held Nelson Mandela."

"That is fair."

"There are two countries we could visit now," Dora said.

"Which ones?"

"South Africa and Myanmar."

"Well I know South Africa, but Myanmar?" Fanny conceded.

"It's what used to be called Burma."

"How exotic!"

"There is an argument around whether you should visit a country -- it is not the regime but the people of the country you wish to visit." Dora reflected.

"I never knew you were so focused on human rights, Dora," Fanny said with a new respect.

"Always have been: I have memberships to most human rights groups, but have never done anything actually. I guess you could say that I am an armchair human rights activist."

"Well it sounds like you have thought long and hard about a lot of issues and I respect you for that."

"Right then, we have a cemetery to find," Dora concluded, and with that the coffee and the conversation were over.

❦ ❦ ❦

Fanny was not into visiting graveyards. They were for families that had buried loved ones, and she was also secretly disturbed that she might see a ghost or two, which would be most unwelcome. The more she thought about it, the more she realised that they would probably walk among the various graves, the little mounds of earth with a headstone or a simple cross, quickly find what they were looking for and leave. What she found was not what she had been expecting. All of the tombs were above ground in these mausoleums with beautiful stonework. In some cases, the graves looked like works of art with the carved figures and images rising up into the sky. Where Fanny had thought she would be in a large open field, instead she was now in a maze of buildings on either side, and this terrified her.

"Dora," Fanny said, "these are very different to our graveyards."

"Yes, they are," she replied. "These are like their own little buildings for the deceased. And many families are all buried within one tomb."

"Well, let's be quick, please," Fanny whispered.

"Come on, this will be fun." Dora quipped.

Fanny edged closer to Dora and hung on to her for dear life.

"Any idea where Eva is buried?" Fanny asked, as the overall size of the cemetery was overwhelming.

"I have a rough idea," Dora replied, "I printed off a map of the cemetery which would make the tomb easier to locate."

"Right then," Fanny mechanically said, not letting go of Dora's arm.

"She is buried with the Duarte family, so we need to find the tomb with the family name on it." With that, Dora extracted the map from her bag, extracted herself from Fanny and looked around, trying to find some landmarks she could use.

Dora lined up her map to get the necessary direction and bearings and then, showing Fanny the rough route, slowly started navigating the maze of stone epitaphs and angel sculptures.

Fanny looked on in disbelief at the various buildings around her and the effort that must have gone into the construction of them. She wanted to take some pictures of the statues but wasn't sure if this was respectful or not.

"Dora," she said, "do you think it is okay if I photograph the tombs."

"I don't see why not," Dora replied, pointing behind and ahead, "everyone else seems to be doing it."

"Well, because others are doing it doesn't mean that I should necessarily," this was said with a bit of annoyance.

"Well then, decide for yourself. Right then," Dora protested and marched ahead.

Fanny looked to her left and right, expecting a long departed soul to chide her, but she took out her phone and started snapping away at a stone carving of an angel which had caught the sunlight and was shining. She marvelled at the beauty of the carving and the sheer size of it. Someone would have had to sit and carve this, consider each and every detail and then make sure that there were no errors – A fine work of art indeed.

When she looked around, she expected to see Dora up ahead but she was not. In fact there was no one within her sights at all. She walked quickly in the direction Dora had taken but couldn't see her down any of the side paths. She had now started to panic as there was no way she wanted to walk through a graveyard on her own, let alone one in which the bodies were housed above ground, ready to attack.

"Bloody hell," she whispered in sheer panic.

Breathe, Fanny, breathe, she kept telling herself. It was then that she came face to face with another visitor. She jumped back in fright and screamed at the top of her lungs, causing the poor woman, who was carrying flowers, to drop them, turn on her heels and run.

"Sorry," Fanny shouted after her, "I just got a terrible fright. So sorry…"

It must have been the commotion which caused Dora's return, for within no time she was next to Fanny, looking her over with a worried expression and concern, "What happened, Fanny?"

"Nothing, dear," Fanny replied, "got the fright of my life, but not to worry."

Lying scattered in front of them were an assortment of flowers. The image was simply beautiful with the tombs surrounding it and it was Dora who proclaimed, "Would make a spectacular picture."

With that, Fanny was snapping pictures and seemed to forget about the ordeal that had previously absorbed her.

"Right then," Dora declared, "it's time to find the Duarte family grave."

Unlike before, Fanny made sure to follow Dora. She was not going to be left alone in this place again.

They knew when they had found the correct tomb, as a throng of people had surrounded it and there were fresh flowers carefully placed there.

Fanny was not sure why Dora wanted to come and see this as other than a small plaque indicating the inhabitant of the tomb there was nothing else. However, it must have meant something to her and she watched as Dora peered into the tomb and carefully read all she could.

"I think this tells us that every place is unique," Dora said. "Some people loved her, others hated her. What if she was lucky enough to live? Would she have been remembered in the same way? But we don't live in a world of 'what ifs' now, do we?"

This seemed to be all they needed to do here, as Dora and Fanny made their way back to the entrance of the cemetery in silence.

❁ ❁ ❁

"We still have some time before our outing this evening, why don't we go to La Boca?"

"Yes, viva La Loca?"

"La Boca - Argentina!" Dora shot back, acknowledging that the joke was on her. Everyone in the village drooled when they thought about the 'handsomest' main in the whole world - Ricky Martin. "It's a colourful part of town where the buildings are painted bright colours and there is a sense of art on the streets."

Fanny quickly wondered if there was anything Dora would gain from going there, a new found passion that would need to be expressed on the streets. She cautiously asked, "Is there anything specific that you want to see there?"

"No," Dora lazily said, "thought we could wander around the streets and maybe have another coffee, and if there is something fascinating to see then go and look."

Fanny felt relieved, as this indicated that there should be nothing to worry about by going out with Dora.

Dora was not joking about the colour. When they got out of the taxi, they were bombarded with colours, bright blue, red and yellow adorned the buildings with some having all three colours. The windows were painted one colour, the doorway another and sometimes even floors were differentiated by colours.

"My word," Fanny said, "would not like their paint bill." At which she then laughed.

"Well, let's say that it is festive, that would be the best way to describe it." Dora added.

In the taxi Dora had lectured her on the prices in this part of town. "We are not buying anything; remember what we agreed before we left, we were not going to buy silly souvenirs, and this place is a magnet for exactly that. And yes, I will be watching you," Dora had said this as her eyes amplified and the look of the matron returned.

"Right then," Fanny responded, expecting herself to say exactly those words. After all had she not been pre-programmed to do this?

And the streets were lined with shops selling paintings and handmade crafts which Fanny was trying hard not to look at, so that there would be no temptation.

It was going to be Christmas the following week and there were various ornaments and decorative items in the shops. How she wanted to buy something to decorate the table of wherever they were going to end up spending Christmas!

"Dora…" she started.

"Yes," came the reply.

"Don't you think it would be a good idea to buy some decorations for our Christmas lunch? Have something to be able to celebrate this time of the year?"

She did not even get a response, and she knew that this was not open to discussion.

They ended up sitting at a cafe in the middle of the area drinking their coffee. Fanny was waiting for the philosophical discussion point on undernourished racoons from the Antarctic, or pop singers who were actually clones, but nothing came. It was as if Dora was simply in a state of being and enjoying all that surrounded her.

❋ ❋ ❋

It didn't take long for Fanny's fears to be once again alerted that something may indeed be up. For supper, they were going to dinner and a Tango show. This simply spelt disaster. Dora had insisted that they go to a very specific tango show, which was a little more modern than the others, and played out near a warehouse district. What made the issue more contentious was that Dora had said in the taxi on the way over that all her life she had wished she had taken up dancing lessons and that this was something she now regretted. *Hmmm*, was all that Fanny could think, as no words wanted to come out.

She could pretend she was feeling ill, but it was Dora who wanted to see the Tango show and so, rather reluctantly, she decided to talk herself into going, and whether she liked it or not she was in a taxi driving through the streets of Buenos Aires and it would be too late to pull out at this stage.

The tango venue was very sleek and modern and the wood shone, as it had been polished to perfection. Fanny was wondering, with wood this shiny, did it not make it slippery for the dancers?

Prior to the show starting, they were fed a steak the size of a tennis court. There was no way that she would be able to eat all of that. The waiter smiled at her throughout the meal and even winked at her when she mentioned the size of the meat.

He was dishy, but a hundred years younger than her. Naughty, naughty man!

The show started with much pomp and ceremony. The music swept through the restaurant and the dancers moved about in between the tables as well as on the stage. Then, the moment that Fanny would remember the most, was when the lights went out completely. One spotlight was trained on two dancers in the middle of the room and so began the complicated tango dance. The man led, the woman responded, (the complicated footwork at that time was all that one could focus on) only to then switch, as the man pushed the woman, who unwound herself and went flying across the floor, to land in perfect harmony and balance.

Fanny not only watched the show, she was watching Dora as well. Her greatest fear was that at some point Dora would be joining in and like the previous experience, she would have to climb under a tree and plant herself with some perennial flowers.

The show continued and the music was more passionate, more intense, and now, instead of the two dancers there were more twirling around, completely enraptured by the dance. Fanny was simply loving it, even though there was a potential threat looming.

During a break between the two sets Dora said, "Simply classic, such form, such poise, such perfection."

"Yes," Fanny said, not wanting to commit to too much conversation.

"You can see these people using this dance form to express themselves, their love, their passion."

"Hmmuh," is all that came out.

Dora nodded and ate her dessert.

The second set was even more complicated, with one dancer, the female, responding to the music and being observed by the other dancer, the male. She basically did the dance for him and spun and performed which made Fanny want to jump to her feet in admiration.

It was as they were coming to the end of the show that all the lights went on and before she knew it the waiter had her on her feet and ready to dance. "No, no…" she protested with her voice, but not her body.

"Relax," was the only word he said, and with that, he winked at her and they were off.

Other waiters had grabbed other diners and the dance began as they were marched and moved, and Fanny felt like she was flying. Not being the smallest of people, she was amazed at how he was able to make her move effortlessly around. She hoped that the dance would never end and around and around she turned. It was over too soon and she was back in her chair staring at Dora who patted her with a napkin.

"Fanny," Dora said while fanning her with the cut-out promoting wine, "your face was simply electric! You seemed to be having so much fun."

"I was," Fanny replied.

"I don't know how you did it," Dora continued, "but you seemed to live the Tango on that floor, you are a complete natural."

With that, Fanny beamed a smile and sat back enjoying the cool air being forced over her and the experience which played in her mind.

"Oooh and don't worry, I got lots of photographs. One even really close up – when you were squashed against the face of the waiter here, before he twirled you over there."

Fanny clawed to get the phone and look at the pictures and saw what Dora meant, the person in the pictures did not seem to be her at all. Instead there was someone who had diamonds sparkling in her eyes and who did not look uncomfortable at all, someone who was living life.

The waiter returned and handed her a small box of chocolates and kissed her hand.

"Thank you," she said to him and squeezed his hand.

"The pleasure was mine." He saw them to their taxi and was still waving as they pulled away.

Fanny turned to Dora and said, "Bloody hell!" The smile that was plastered all over her face looked very different to anything that had come before.

Chapter Twelve
Argentina
-San Carlos de Bariloche

Fanny was not looking forward to being stuck in a bus overnight, as Dora had indicated. This would mean a repeat of the experience on the aeroplane, with the only bonus being that one was able to get out when the bus stopped for routine breaks. Fanny wanted to protest but then realised it was futile, as this was one of those moments that made this kind of trip cost-effective.

Unlike the previous ticket buying experience, it was Dora who bought the tickets for their next bus journey. "Two tickets to Rio Negro, please. We are going to San Carlos de Bariloche." The women behind the counter didn't even look up, printed the tickets, showed her the amount and grabbed the notes before counting them and returning the change.

No directions of where to go were given. Dora was not one to take this lying down and she pointed at herself, "Customer. You seller, you be nice. I can choose to be nice because I am customer."

Fanny could not quite believe what she was hearing, but there was no doubt that Dora was not taking on this rudeness.

"Now, where do we go for the bus?" Dora asked with a strained civility.

The woman, shocked at the preceding events, pointed towards the door at the end of the passage and indicated right.

"Thank you," Dora said.

They made their way out of the terminus and to where the buses were situated. They looked carefully for the name of the town on their bus and waited patiently.

"It's going to be a long ride, we had better brace ourselves for the worst."

Fanny thought differently. "It's time for some relaxation and rest. A bus ride is a good time to sit and think. We have been going now for all this time and we need to have some down time."

"Fair enough," Dora said. "Bariloche, is that for us too?"

The doors of the bus opened and they were met with a kind face. They showed their tickets, had their luggage stored and were given the most wonderful seats, which were located in the top section of the bus. These weren't ordinary bus seats, they were full-on business class bus seats.

Fanny could not believe her luck. It was too good to be true.

The seats could recline to make a bed, and as Dora and Fanny fell into them, they knew that even though the journey might take 24 hours, it was going to be comfortable.

They were even given a welcome pack and a generous smile from both the driver and the bus steward.

As they left Buenos Aires behind them, Fanny thought about the experience from the night before. Dora thought of the mausoleum of Eva and both drifted off to sleep as they enjoyed being able to recline their seats into beds and feel the gentle humming of the bus's engine.

When Fanny woke up her hair was crazy, not to mention that her face felt like it was dented. It took her a few seconds to orient herself and she couldn't quite seem to be able to place where she was. In the seat across from hers Dora was sitting up and writing in her journal. She looked like she normally did – a picture of perfection.

"Morning," she muttered to her.

Dora looked up and could not help it, "Now is a good time for a 'selfie'!"

"Funny," she mumbled.

As she looked out the window next to her she was struck by the rawness of the countryside.

"Still another six hours," Dora commented and with that, Fanny fell back into her makeshift bed and closed her eyes.

❀ ❀ ❀

San Carlos de Bariloche did look like a Swiss country town and even though this was summer, she could imagine how it must look in the winter time.

Their hotel overlooked the blue lake below and the mountains peeked out of the clouds in the distance. They were not hikers, so they would not be climbing these mountains; instead they would use the three days they were going to be there to have some much needed relaxation and, of course, celebrate Christmas.

It was completely strange to have Christmas in summer, not that it was sweltering hot, but the sun was out, there was no snow outside and unlike in the United Kingdom there were not any overly decorated Christmas displays everywhere you looked.

The way Christmas was celebrated in Argentina was to have a Christmas Eve dinner. For their dinner, Dora had booked them at the hotel restaurant. It was going to be fun, not to have to do the cooking and instead sit back and be served. It would also be great that there would be no irritating extended family with their even more irritating children, Fanny strategically thought.

❀ ❀ ❀

A Christmas dinner had not been this much fun in ages, with people from all around Bariloche arriving to celebrate with their families. All those that were family-less were included in the celebrations, which had a barbecue section as well as the usual roasts.

The plates were piled high with food, the conversation buzzed around them and they were warmly greeted by all those that walked past, "*Buenas noches.*"

"*Buenas noches,*" was their reply, as well as, "*Feliz Navidad.*"

The waiter was sure to mention that they needed to stay up until midnight to see in the Christmas day. "Oh, no," Dora replied, "we simply couldn't, but it would be a lovely idea."

"In Argentina, we do something very different. You will not regret it," he said.

Dora looked to Fanny, "Are you up for it?"

"Of course I am," she replied.

"Right then," Dora said, and ordered another coffee.

Before midnight they were lead outside by a whole group of people and stood looking over the lake in front of them. It was then that all around them people started to light paper decorations, which were then sent into the evening sky.

"What are those?" Dora asked the family next to her, pointing at the decoration.

The man, unable to speak English, but understanding what she meant, said, "*Globos.*"

It was mesmerising, the lake, the lights dotting around and being reflected within it. The sound of happiness as people together enjoyed the beauty of a holiday that allowed them to be humans in touch with each other.

❀ ❀ ❀

Dora had thought it would be best to meet in the lounge area first before breakfast. Fanny was secretly pleased, as she had a surprise for Dora and was going to spring it on her when she got there.

She extracted the bust of Eva Peron that she had found in a shop in Buenos Aires. That made it sound like she had secretly walked into a shop and bought it, with all the time in the world, which was far from the reality. She had seen it every morning as they had left their hotel and made their way up to the main road on which they would then take public transport or a taxi. She couldn't believe how dainty and startling it was. Dora had not noticed it once during the entire stay and Fanny thought she should enquire about the price.

While pretending to have an afternoon rest, she had scouted the corridors to make sure Dora was not prowling and slipped out of the hotel praying that she would go undetected.

She arrived at the shop and it seemed like the lady behind the counter was waiting for her. She walked over to the statue, raised it up and showed Fanny the price, which was reasonable. Fanny handed over the cash, as simply as that. It was then carefully wrapped by the lady, who put some bubble thingies on it, paper wrapped it and included every other kind of wrapping one could to it.

With that she thanked her profusely and snuck back into the hotel. She thought it was going to be an easy slip back in, but how wrong she was! At the front desk was none other than Dora, in full swing with the concierge, "Now should we consider the modern version of the tango show or a more classical one, what would you suggest?"

She stopped dead in her tracks, unable to breathe, and yet very aware that her larger frame had already made it mostly into the reception area. Raising the package to the same level as her face she quickly charged for the elevator and managed to push the button while the voice rang out, "Tango is so passionate, I want to make sure I experience the best kind of passion that one can." Chortle, chortle.

She had carried the gift from Buenos Aires to here, carefully placing it in her luggage and making sure that the suitcase squeezed closed as it was now overfull.

She couldn't wait to see Dora's face. Either she was going to be really happy and thank her or she would lecture her about the fact that they were not going to buy anything on the trip and leave the statue behind. She was feeling the latter really might be the one that Dora would pursue, but something she was learning on this trip was that if she wanted to do something, she would. And if need be they could then send it by mail all the way home.

She carefully extracted the wrapped gift from her bag and placed it carefully in a gift folder and then closed her door and made her way to the lounge which overlooked the lake.

Fanny was happy to see that Dora was already sitting waiting and loudly said, "Merry Christmas, Dora, dear friend."

Dora stood up and flung her arms around her, "Merry Christmas, Fanny."

While they were still standing, Fanny, who could not wait any longer, transferred the gift into Dora's hand. "Don't be mad with me, I know we said no gifts and no things, but I had to."

There was a tear in Dora's eye when she looked at the wrapped gift in her hand. "Fanny, thank you." Fanny, expecting her to open the gift immediately, was surprised when she leaned down to the sofa and extracted another wrapped gift which had been lying there and lifted it and gave it to her.

"Here, I was worried you would be angry with me because I had bought you a gift," Dora said, looking visibly relieved.

"Dora," Fanny said, "You naughty girl."

Both had a good giggle before sitting down to open their respective gifts.

Fanny was wondering whatever it could be.

They both delicately undid the packaging, careful not to seem over eager, even though they desperately wanted to see what each gift held.

Fanny was able to get to her gift first and looked at the box completely confused, even though she knew she was supposed to be grateful.

The picture on the box displayed a long pole-like object which people were holding and smiling. Well it was the thought that counts, and she opened it to look even more confused at the actual pole thingy inside.

Dora on the other hand had extracted the statue and there was a tear running down her cheek as she gently touched it carefully like it was made of gold and she had just won the jackpot.

"Fanny…" she stuttered, but then could not say more as the tears continued to come.

Fanny was pleased that she had made such an impact on her friend and, feeling all festive, squeezed Dora's shoulder.

After some time of marvelling at the statue Dora carefully placed it on the table in front of her. "Do you like your gift, Fanny?"

Fanny was not sure of what to say and smiled at Dora, that smile, and said, "Thank you."

"Well then, why aren't you using it, we should be using it right now."

"Should we?" Fanny asked, trying to keep control of her smile, knowing full well that confusion was starting to spread all over her face.

"Come, let me show you how." Dora had rescued the pole from her and then said, "Give me the phone."

Fanny was worried. It seemed like Dora had bought this pole to smash her phone because she was taking too many photographs and this was starting to irritate her. She didn't want to hand it over. Dora looked at her intently and as always, she became Pavlovian and found her hands moving towards the phone, picking it up and handing it over to her, even though her mind was shouting *No, don't do it, you have rights!*

Dora carefully took the phone and placed it in a compartment on the pole thingy. It clicked in and Dora was delighted. "There we are, wasn't that easy?"

Fanny continued to smile and show her teeth, not knowing what she should say. "Thank you, Dora."

"Well come on, try it," Dora instructed.

"Well it's resting, isn't it," Fanny said to which Dora's right eyebrow raised dangerously.

"All right, let me show you the wonders of the 'selfie stick'," Dora said, excited. "You switch on the camera function and then you do a front lens, and then you look, you see, you hold it in the distance like this, and we can take a 'selfie' with more depth so that it actually looks like someone else is taking the picture."

Fanny could not believe her eyes and looked on in sheer amazement. What was unfolding in front of her? The smile was quickly wiped off her face and was replaced with an open mouth, which, if left for too long, would induce a drool-like action.

"Now you try," Dora said, handing over the 'selfie stick' to her.

Fanny felt both of her hands reaching heavenward to receive the contraption. She looked at it in wonder and just like Dora had touched the statue, she felt her fingers running carefully over each part of the contraption and smiling, smiling like a super model in a bread factory.

"Dora, I can't thank you enough," she said, still not letting go of the 'selfie' stick.

"Right then," Dora said, "we need a picture of us and the lake and my statue. Then we need breakfast and then we can take a walk along the lake? Sound good?"

"Sounds marvellous," Fanny responded, and with that she carefully placed herself next to Dora lined up for the 'selfie' with her new stick and took an iconic photograph with the mountain, a blue lake and the most beautiful background.

The walk was spectacular as they were able to breathe in the fresh country air, enjoy the tranquillity of the lake, deserted on this Christmas day and mostly look towards the warm summer's sun, a novelty to them both.

❋ ❋ ❋

As they were going to be spending a few more days on the lake, they thought that all business would be closed on Boxing day, how wrong they were, because there was no such thing in Argentina, which meant that the two friends could go into town to sample the various chocolates and other delicacies.

They wandered around the streets with the wooden buildings, which reminded them of pictures of Switzerland.

And sample the chocolates they did. Even if they had eaten a small village the night before, Fanny was keen to try all the different variations and flavours of chocolate that she could. From nuts to chillies to caramel, all of it was somehow mixed together ready to be digested!

The rest of the time was spent reading in the lounge overlooking the lake and allowing the relaxation of the countryside to penetrate them, restore them for the next round of adventures.

❋ ❋ ❋

Dora and Fanny had been looking forward to the lake crossing from Argentina to Chile, as it involved a day of moving across the three lakes that were en route from one country to the next. It would allow them to appreciate the Andes mountains from the various boats they were about to go on, and with a singular unique border crossing between the two countries, without an airport in sight.

It was while they were sailing on the Nahuel Huapi Lake that Dora looked to her and said, "Fanny, we could have been at home, playing bridge, worrying about our neighbours and feeling slightly down. Instead, we are sailing on a lake in Argentina, we are going to spend the day enjoying nature and although we are almost neighbours, I don't think we are fighting." With that, she poked Fanny in the ribs, causing her to expel air at a mighty rate. Chortle, chortle.

"Yes," she said not wanting to be the victim to any more bodily harm.

The movement across the water was perfect and they had simply looked out and not felt the need to have to talk. They moved from one area of the lake to the next and each corner, brought about new views which were even more spectacular than the last.

They were about to stop for lunch overlooking the lake before carrying on in a bus towards the next stop and next lake.

"So, Fanny," Dora said, "I don't know how many countries you have visited, but this is going to be another unique border crossing. Every time I have travelled it has mostly been through an airport, and the idea of leaving a country is so definite. But think about today -- we have meandered over the lakes and mountains from one country to the next and you realise just how silly the idea of country demarcations really is. Yes, there are all the other reasons -- nations, costs and security -- but it's all just land and water, land and water that people tread on. At one point we could do so freely; now we must register, be accounted for, and our difference from the others in that country must be noted. I never thought about it like this, until today when moving about as we have."

Fanny did not respond immediately. "Dora, you are such a philosopher…"

Dora smiled and looked out into the depths of the lake. A long and comfortable silence ensued.

"It's never too late to start a new degree in Philosophy," Fanny said.

Dora smiled and then said, "It would simply get in the way of travel."

The rest of the day they went through more lakes and more mountains, more lakes and mountains, another lake another mountain, and finally passed through the two countries' borders, being bussed from one to the other. During this time Fanny thought about what Dora had said, as the person at each border post picked up her passport looked the photograph intensely, then looked at her, then once more looked at the photograph even more intensely. Had she changed? Was she looking different? Or was it as Dora had noted, a silly ritual to be performed?

Once inside Chile, they continued to the waters of the Todos Los Santos to see the awe-inspiring Mount Puntiagudo and Osorno volcano. It was something outside of a film and the new 'selfie' stick was used in overtime as Dora and Fanny posed alongside the water, the volcano and the blue sky beyond. At one point Dora wanted to go and find her statue to include it in the photographs and it was Fanny who talked her out of it.

"We don't want it damaged, now, do we?" Fanny had said reassuringly.

"I guess so," Dora had said while pouting.

"There will be plenty of other opportunities to include Eva on our travels, I promise," Fanny said, before distracting Dora with a "…smile, Dora, smile."

By the time they drove into Puerto Montt they were exhausted by the day that had preceded them.

"We can stay here in Puerto Montt for the night or live dangerously and catch a bus to Santiago. What is it going to be?" Dora asked.

"I don't know, part of me wants to keep on going and thinks catching the bus is a good idea. The other part of me says, shouldn't we stop and have a look at what Puerto Montt has to offer? I don't actually know."

"There are those that visit a single city for ten days, those that visit a few cities or towns within a country, those that get a taste of a few countries; there are no rules, each one has its benefits and I would be happy to do any kind. John and Jong liked travelling this way that we are doing. I have visited Paris for two weeks, only leaving it to go to Versailles. There are no rules to travel, that's the rule."

Fanny shot a look at Dora and then said, "Well then, let's get those tickets to Santiago!"

With that, the two made their way to the local bus station with Fanny insisting on buying the tickets this time. The last thing the poor bus ticket sales person needed was a lecture!

Two tickets bound for Santiago, Chile were in hand, and as they boarded the bus, even though they had left Argentina a long time before this, Dora turned, and said, "Don't cry for me Argentina." Fanny was quite aware that no tears were going to be shed but decided to say nothing. Sometimes things are best left unsaid, or, even better, sometimes it is best to:

Let sleeping elderly women lie!

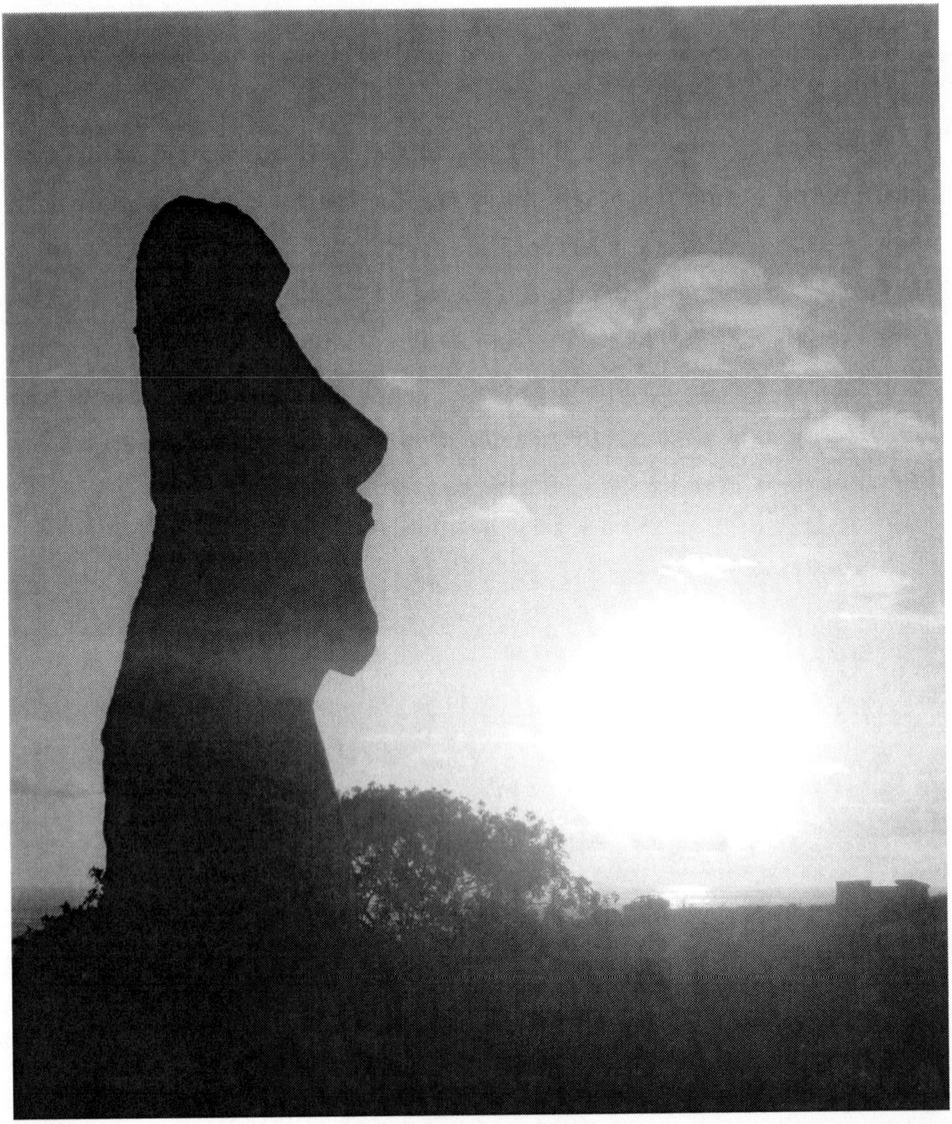

Part Four ~
The place that time forgot, or, simply put: show me the Easter Bunny

There are so many voices in my head, so so so so so many!!!! Help!!!!! Not only is the book stolen and written under another bloody author but now even the characters are plotting against me. I don't exist, maybe I really don't exist. Helllllpppppp!!!!! →

Chapter Thirteen
~~Chile~~ Easter Island
-Easter Island

You can't start a new section of the book here," Dora said.
"Of course I bloody can," Fanny responded.
"Language, we spoke about language," Dora reminded her. *"Easter Island is part of Chile, so it can't have its own section, it should be under the Chile section."*
"But it's another bloody place all together…"
"Language…"
"Who's writing this book, you or me?"
"You, but I thought I would help with the correct technical issues."
"Easter Island is getting its own section!" And that was the end of the discussion. Fanny was in control!

"**B**loody hell," Fanny's voice protested loudly through the air. "We are travelling five hours into the middle of nowhere to go and visit an island where the Easter Bunny comes from; that's just wrong!"

"Not where the Easter Bunny comes from, it's called Easter Island…Never mind," Dora said, upset. "We are going to see the *stupas* on the island, the famous rock carvings."

"We could see stupid things in many places in the United Kingdom, my dear," Fanny responded, rather dismally.

"*Stupas* are not the same as stupid."

"Enlighten me," Fanny said.

"A *stupa* is a statue, a symbolic one normally associated with a religious group," Dora pointed out, "and Easter Island has a combination of them, which are filled with mystery, considering the size and location of many of them."

"Sounds fascinating." The voice was flat and lifeless and Fanny was not trying to pretend that the statement was not thick with sarcasm.

Dora, however, knew exactly what to say and had waited strategically for this time. "Photographers have said that photographing the *stupas* has been one of the highlights, not only of a trip to South America, but of their lives. One man likened it to touching the face of Michael Jackson."

The word 'photograph' was all that was necessary. Fanny's ears had pricked up at that sound alone, and she imagined that if she was a cartoon character her eyes would literally have stood out at a 90-degree angle.

"It's only five hours," she heard herself say, as she gently massaged the pocket where her phone was located, still without a sim card, and the 'selfie' stick which she had strapped to her backpack for easy access.

The flight was on the national carrier and just before they landed, Fanny was able to make out the following statement, in broken English, "The runaway is a beeeeet shorrrttt. So...the landeeeeeenngggg will be a littlleeeee bit queeeckkkkk."

She leaned over to Dora and half-jokingly said, "Didn't really understand all of that, but it almost sounded like we would be in for a rough landing. Amazing what one hears through it all, I must be wrong."

"No, that is what I heard too." Dora confirmed.

"Bloooodddddyyyyyy heeeelllllllll," were the last words that Dora heard from Fanny, because for the remainder of the descent and final approach she was hyperventilating into the air sickness bag.

The captain wasn't joking either, because they managed to land and halt within seconds. Fanny used up every opportunity for drama, making a rasping noise as they hit the tarmac and allowing her entire body to be taken with the force. She let out a scream -- well, not really a scream, but more like the sound of indigestion coupled with the sounds singers make when they warm up.

Dora looked stoically ahead and although her eyes were a little concerned, her face was typically British. She was doing this for Queen and country.

"Doraaaaaaaaa," Fanny choked, "we are not going back in a plane."

Dora looked over at this point, nodded and said, "Well then, I guess we will become inhabitants of Easter Island."

The matter was never brought up again.

Once they left the airport building, what had been a stressful arrival turned into something quite different.

They saw their names on a board being held by a woman with a kind face. Dora walked over and said, "Hello. That's us."

"Welcome, welcome," the woman beamed, and before they knew it, they were each wearing a garland of flowers around their necks.

"It is our pleasure to welcome you to Easter Island, or Rapa Nui as we call it."

"Thank you," they said in unison.

The flowers were pink and yellow and Fanny had her phone out in no time taking pictures, even at one point pulling out the 'selfie' stick to ensure that she got a picture with all three of them.

"It is a little ride to the guest house," she said, and in no time they were bouncing their way through the streets of Hang Roa.

For somewhere so remote Fanny was amazed at how much it looked like any normal small town. She was not sure what to expect, but they even passed coffee shops, restaurants and little grocery places. Sometimes people can really have the wrong idea, she thought, pointing the finger directly at herself.

When they finally arrived at the guest house, what greeted them was something even more bizarre. They were staying in the main building but dotted all over the grassy area in front of them were tents where other people were staying. And there, not even 20 metres from the camp site, stood a *stupa*, towering over the peninsula it protected.

Fanny did not even retrieve her bags from the vehicle; she was out walking briskly towards it. This 'selfie' could not wait.

❀ ❀ ❀

Dora and Fanny stood over the bicycle. Fanny was a little more animated, looking at it with fascination.

"Right then, let's hire them," Fanny said, with a significant amount of enthusiasm.

"I don't think that is a good idea," Dora replied, with a puzzled look on her face.

"Why ever not?"

"Well…" Dora began, but then looked away, then up, then to the side and then back to Fanny. "You are not a fan of too much exercise."

"Bloody hell," Fanny replied, "this island is flat and it's not like we are going to cycle back to the mainland!"

Dora smiled and looked at her friend, constantly surprised by the ongoing new opportunities to look at her differently. "Well then, in your or my words, because they have become intertwined, right then, let's hire!"

The sight was comic indeed: two women with grey hair, one tall and one round, buzzing along the roads and pathways of the town. Dora was expecting that Fanny would struggle, but there were no complaints, and it was Dora who was out of breath while Fanny maintained a constant pace.

At one point they had coffee overlooking the small harbour and another time they stopped to take a look at one of the Moai statues close to the town.

When they made it back to their guest house they were amazed at how many people were staying, as the tents had been pitched but the inhabitants not identified. There was a buzz around the various seating areas and a large group of Japanese students had a guitar and were singing away at the top of their lungs. When they saw Fanny and Dora they beckoned them over to join them.

"Oh, no dear," Dora heard Fanny say, "I am not much of a singer."

"But I am," Dora said with much excitement.

That was all the group needed to hear, and soon they were chanting, "Sit, sit, sit!"

Fanny and Dora did what they were told, with a certain smile escaping onto Fanny's face.

"You have such kind face," the voice said, and Fanny looked next to her and saw a small Japanese girl and her smile beaming up at her.

"Oh, that is very kind, dear, but as I said, I am not much of a singer."

"We are all singer," was the response.

Fanny felt the smile tighten around her lips and her inner voice decided to say, *That is a fallacy my dear, because some of us really should not be singing!* She jumped back in fright because this time it felt too real, and she was convinced that everyone must have heard it. However, there was that gentle smile, and the eyes still looked up kindly at her.

Then, to everyone's delight, the guitarist started to strum the notes to "Hey Jude," and Dora let out a little scream, which got the group even more excited. Well, at least they weren't going to be killing Argentina slowly and painfully.

Fanny even found herself singing along; not that she knew the words well but the chorus was infectious. There, people from all over the world were singing together on an island in the middle of nowhere and Dora's voice was not breaking glasses this time, as there was a joint voice rising into the night sky.

Later, when the group has stopped singing, Fanny and Dora had found a new friend, "Tamika from Tokyo."

Dora, ever pragmatic, said, "Please spell it for me and then let me know how to pronounce it so that I say it correctly. I am so happy to have a friend from Japan."

"T-A-M-I-K-A."

Fanny and Dora listened carefully and then both had a chance to say, "Nice to meet you, Tamika."

"Nice to meet you, too." The smile was perfection.

"You have the most gracious smile," Dora said.

Tamika did not say anything but continued to smile back.

Fanny, eager to ensure that she was a part of the conversation, asked, "How long have you been on Easter Island?"

"Two days," came the reply.

"So, almost as long as us," Fanny chortled.

"Naughty girl," Dora exclaimed at the joke, and play-smacked her hand.

Tamika watched in awe and said, "I think we travel together."

"Travel together?" They both responded.

"Yes, we can hire car and travel together on island," Tamika said.

"Oh that is very kind of you to offer to drive," Fanny said. They had wondered how they were going to get to the more remote parts of the island.

"No, I don't have licence."

"Oh, I see," Fanny said, "nor do we."

"I do," Dora said.

"Don't joke, Dora," Fanny said, "I can't imagine you behind the wheel of a car in a foreign country which is completely different to ours."

Dora raised her eyebrow. "It's not a spaceship Fanny, it's simply a vehicle which needs to be driven, and in case you haven't noticed, there is only normally one car on the road at any time!"

Fanny let out a deflated laugh and then, when she realised that Dora was being serious, went slowly mute.

Dora looked at Tamika and asked, "Do you know where we can hire a car?"

Tamika was about to respond when Fanny, worrying that the conversation was getting out of control, cut in and said, "I think a tour is the sensible thing to do." Then, with a smile that was transformed into a grimace and then back into a smile and then a snarl, "…that way we can all take pictures." Her eyes moved rapidly from Tamika to Dora and back again.

Dora looked past her to Tamika -- clearly a new alliance had been built in record time -- and said, "Carry on Tamika."

"In town," Tamika responded, her eyes lighting up.

"Well then, it is a trip to town tomorrow to go and get a vehicle!"

❀ ❀ ❀

Fanny clutched her fingers around the safety belt that was strapped around her waist. This was simply not cricket, it was like one of those wild thingamajigs at the fair where people bumped and jumped and fell around, followed by the one child or adult (mostly adult) running towards the bathroom and not making it on time (unfortunately), and leaving their breakfast on the floor for all to see! Except that this time, it was the roads which would be called rustic or rural being navigated by Dora, who was not used to them, which meant that they fell from one hole into another.

Tamika, on the other hand, was quite calm. Fanny could attest to this as she had brought down the sun shade to look in its mirror to see if she was still in the vehicle and had not fallen out, but she was sitting calmly with her camera in hand, a large Japanese one almost the same size as her, looking out at the scenery. In her other hand she held the map of the island, as well as a short history of each site that they would visit over the two days.

Dora's face was a picture of determination as her eyes bore into the road in front of her. *Bloody hell,* Fanny thought, in that voice that talked to her.

Tamika had recommended a route based on the layout of the island, but then had said something which had gotten them all excited. "Tomorrow, New Year!"

"Well, it is," Dora had responded.

"So, tomorrow we wake up early and watch the sun rise."

Fanny stared in horror as she could not think of herself dying on the first day of a new year on the roughest roads in the world. Surely, Dora would not want to do this? It screamed of silliness.

"What a wonderful idea, Tamika," Dora shot back enthusiastically, "you are such a marvel at interesting experiences."

Tamika beamed, "We go to the Ahu Tongariki site. Perfect to watch sun rise, and we see the Moai statues at same time."

It was Dora who had lit up like those cheap Christmas lights and raised her hands off the steering wheel. "Yay, I am so excited!"

Fanny could not believe her ears. "It will be dark," she said.

"Even more fun," Dora chirped.

Fanny had dug her fingers even harder into the safety belt and watched as they turned purple from the pressure.

When the vehicle did eventually come to a stop, it took both Dora and Tamika to pry Fanny's fingers off the seatbelt and to help her out of the car. Dora rolled her eyes at Tamika and Tamika tried to look serious but could not help displaying a small smile. Fanny saw this and was not pleased. It seemed like she was not a part of this, something which would need to be sorted out soon. However, she did not feel like talking at this point and simply followed the two, partially hypnotised.

In front of them, there where they had parked, not far in the distance, was the crater of a volcano. Fanny simply stared in disbelief. *The Fanny of the rising sun, the Fanny of the picture wars, the Fanny of I click -- her smile was not doing anything but staring*, not that a smile can stare! Dora looked at her in alarm. Two fingers quickly were raised in front of her eyes and two loud clicks later and Fanny came out of her trance.

"Bloody hell," she said.

"Thought we had lost you there for a second," Dora said, and with that, she marched towards the edge of the crater where Tamika was taking pictures of the mesmerising scene below.

Fanny could feel herself returning to normalcy as she went for her phone and started to take pictures too.

"Volcanoes always fascinate me; to think that there, underneath the surface are fire and molten lava which live in some harmony until they can't anymore, and then explode heavenward, roaring and yelling in an angry march up there." Dora was animated as she said this, her hands chartering the flow of the lava and the movement upwards.

Tamika stared at the visual explanation and then said, "You speak like poetry…I listen to you all time."

This was all that Dora needed as she looked upwards, then downwards and then drew her hands back to her sides, while doing a half bow.

Tamika, absolutely delighted, clapped her hands and blew kisses at Dora, whose normally stern features were replaced with a smile.

"You speak tonight at New Year's Party," Tamika said.

"New Year's Party?" Fanny responded in a rising voice.

"Yes, at guest house," Tamika replied, "all guest party together tonight to say goodbye to old year and hello to new one."

"No, dear," Fanny said mechanically, "we wouldn't be welcome, we are older, you know."

"No, no," Tamika quickly said, "all people welcome."

Dora continued to smile and Fanny got that sinking feeling in the pit of her stomach. Either they were going to have a singing contest or poetry. And she didn't even drink, so she would not be able to use that as an excuse. Fanny was wondering how to get out of this one, only to be met with the absolute horror of her worst nightmare confirmed.

"You speak tonight at party," she said to Dora while giving her a small hug from the side.

Dora did not say anything in return but continued to beam for the rest of the walk around the crater.

Tamika had been watching Fanny closely as she took pictures and quietly slipped in next to her and with that gentle voice said, "Your photo so good." With this came a thumbs up.

Fanny smiled in return, but Tamika had an ulterior motive. "Do you know how to take panoramic photo?"

"Pana-what dear?" Fanny responded.

"Take photo all the way around," Tamika said imitating moving all the way around.

"No dear, this isn't a fancy camera like your one," Fanny mumbled.

"Can I look?" Tamika asked.

Fanny handed over the phone and raised her hands in surrender.

"I think I show you something," and Tamika carefully moved around doing a full circle. Fanny was intrigued and Tamika bent over and showed her what she had taken. "It's a function on your phone. It take photo all the way around like panorama."

"My word," Fanny said excitedly. "But there is no way I can remember all these little buttons and thingies," this was said with an air of despondency.

"I show you," Tamika said.

Tamika then carefully showed Fanny the various functions, from 'panorama' to 'slo-mo', but drew the line at video because she thought that it was all getting a bit complicated.

After a few attempts, Fanny had mastered the panorama and Tamika found herself posing in photos with the crater and the blue sky beyond.

In the afternoon there were plenty of opportunities to practice, as they went to the quarry where the Moai had been carved, named Rano Raraku, according to Tamika.

As they got out of the car, Dora looked out and started to say, "To be or not be? That is the question..."

Tamika once again applauded in delight. It cut through Fanny like a knife.

While Dora and Tamika weaved through the quarry up and down the hills looking at the various Moai half falling, erect or simply half mast, Fanny walked in a daze, worried about the ensuing drama that would be taking place in the evening.

At one point, she had to smack and remind herself that she was standing in a magical place with thousands of photo opportunities, and although the others were miles ahead of her, she slowly brought out her phone and began the dutiful task of taking photos or 'selfies' or a combination of both.

Before she knew it, there was a picture of the three of them and a large Moai towering above them, and then there were three different faces: one speckled with the hope of a young person and two faces which were painted with the adventure of South America. Fanny beamed in delight at this, this joy of collecting memories in a way which was immediate and real. This was followed dutifully by a panoramic shot.

"Now we can go to place where we see bird man," Tamika motioned back to the car.

"Bird who?" Fanny asked.

"Place where famous bird man is."

"I thought he was in a jail in San Francisco?" Fanny said confused.

"Yes," Dora responded, "there was that movie about Alcatraz and…"

"No," Tamika laughed, and then, worrying that she had offended them, looked down and said, "there is also bird man here, same-same but a little different."

This confused Fanny even more and she had to ask, "Same-same, what dear?"

"The tale of the bird man linked to a contest where man go to swim to island and get egg and then get virgin as prize."

"Sounds deplorable," Fanny said, alarmed.

Dora had even raised her eyebrows in shock.

"Not anymore," Tamika said, getting herself tongue-tied. "Men of island swim to island next door and get egg at top of mountain; whoever come back with egg not broken, get virgin."

"I think it is the virgin thing that worried me," Dora said.

"Yes," Fanny agreed, "this is most worrying."

"What if he was 'that way' and did not want a woman?" Dora said.

Tamika and Fanny looked at Dora, confused.

"Well, don't tell me you didn't find Elton John attractive!"

"What an interesting observation," Fanny said, teeth displayed, and with that they were back in their car to go and look at the site of the contest which had caused so many challenges!

While the three stared over the water to the rocky outcrop where the other island was, Dora smiled as she had reflected on what she had said. Fanny and Tamika were lost in their own thoughts.

"Right then," Dora said, "homeward bound, it's party time…"

This was all that was needed, and Fanny shot Tamika a distressed look, but Tamika was not looking at her, but rather, beaming at the person in front of her.

❆ ❆ ❆

It was quite a spectacle, the two long tables placed at the end of the guest house field which overlooked the ocean and the Moai that had been subjected to the 'selfie' extravaganza on arrival. The sun was slowly setting as the tables were filled with people from the tents and the guest house, people from all around the world, excitedly chatting, introducing themselves and telling stories. Fanny and Dora had been adopted by the Japanese guests and treated like two celebrities, with more 'selfies' taken in one hour than all those young pop stars could ever dream of.

The owner of the guest house had roped in her whole family to help, and there, carrying the trays and beaming at the guests, was a wonderful older woman, who turned out to be the owner's mother, who gently touched their shoulders in solidarity. With her were two younger women, the owner's daughters, and so there were three generations of women bustling about. Then, to everyone's surprise, local music started playing and the dance of the island was being demonstrated to them by these very beautiful women. "It is very similar to Hawaiian dance," Dora exclaimed, only to notice that Fanny was no longer sitting next to her. Fanny had made her way to the edge of the area where they were dancing and was capturing everything.

The applause was thunderous and the screams for encore meant that the dancing went on as people cheered, clapped and celebrated the beauty of the local culture.

In no time, Fanny had a long list of requests from the Japanese guests to please e-mail and Facebook the pictures. Fanny looked on in horror. Tamika could only hug her as the rest of the group were worried they had offended her.

"I show you how to share photo?" Tamika said cautiously.

Fanny let out a laugh and said, "You can show me, my dear, but you will only frustrate yourself. Here, take it and you go for it and share."

Dora looked over in awe at what had just happened; Fanny had surrendered something which could never, never, never have been considered.

Tamika showed Fanny as she clicked and pushed and touched, and Fanny smiled back, but when she looked to Dora, the seat was empty and Dora was gone.

From the shadows came a booming voice and Fanny nearly dropped her phone in fright. "Ladies and Gentleman, a word please…" Dora emerged from behind a post. She had tied a scarf around her head and was walking slowly towards the two tables. Fanny wondered if she should crawl away quickly now.

"It is New Year's Eve and here we are, people from all around the world, sharing our space and time together. I cannot help but be thankful for this wonderful opportunity. I am an older lady, and it is through this experience of travel that I feel young again, so I wanted to say to all of you, enjoy this wonderful time we have."

Everyone had gone quiet and Fanny could feel her insides panic, but what Dora was saying was so lovely that she didn't know how to feel about it.

"May the year ahead be filled with adventure and stories, with the laughter of friends, with the joy of unexplored sites. May each of you have the chance to do something that you always dreamed of and most importantly, may you challenge yourselves in a way that allows you to do something you never dreamed you would do. Over there is my dear friend Fanny, who has come on this journey with me. In our later years, we decided to try something different and it has been simply glorious. May you also have the chance to have a dear friend like her, and if you don't yet have a dear friend, may you have the opportunity to find one. We made a new friend here and her smile has accompanied us in our viewing of these beautiful and haunting statues. To the New Year!"

With that, everyone applauded loudly and the entire Japanese contingent went to hug Dora, but it was Fanny who was stunned as the tears ran down her cheeks.

"Thank you," she said to Dora once the others had finished hugging her, "I am so lucky to have you as a friend."

The food was then brought to the tables and there, under the stars, they sat and ate with each other.

As the night wore on, the excitement of the New Year beckoned, and in no time, there were people dancing about.

Dora was in the lead in one of those dances which required people to hang on behind and follow with their arms attached to the person's hips. Fanny was on the dance floor shuffling about, to the delight of the Japanese travellers who clapped and formed a circle around her.

Then midnight struck and there were more cheers and noise. Dora and Fanny quietly left the party, but not before exchanging a hug and no words. They were going to rest for a few hours before they needed to leave on the sunrise adventure. Tamika, however, was not going to sleep, she had informed them with a wink.

❀ ❀ ❀

"Are you sure this is the correct place? Because all I see is darkness," Fanny protested from the front of the car.

Tamika said calmly, "Yes," as she looked once more at the map using the torch which was strapped to a band which went around her head.

Dora had parked and they all sat inside the vehicle in an uncomfortable silence.

Fanny was about to say something more, when Tamika pointed at another set of headlights which were making their way down the mountain. "More people coming."

Dora opened her door and said, "Well then, let's try and find a nice spot in the dark. Tamika, you are in charge with the torch to show us the way."

Tamika had come prepared, and although she had used a head torch to read, she had other lighting devices to ensure a safe passage to the Moai.

"There," she pointed in the direction of where she thought the Moai were, "is where we should go."

They walked cautiously along as Tamika showed the way. They came up to a site where they could see the rock and platform of what looked like a Moai. "This is Ahu Tongariki, the best place to watch morning sunrise," Tamika informed.

"Well it is very dark now, so maybe the sun won't rise for a long time," Fanny said, sounding disturbed and grumpy from a limited amount of sleep and another treacherous car drive.

"Right then, Fanny, it's all going to be okay." Dora touched her shoulder and then, out of the bag she was carrying, Tamika extracted three little fold-up chairs as well as various foodstuffs she had prepared.

"Breakfast while we wait," she said as she handed over little sandwiches she had made.

Fanny looked in awe at this.

"You are the sweetest ever." Dora said. She tucked into the sandwiches and then watched as more was unpacked, including coffee, treats and some sugary things which were simply delightful.

And while they were munching away the colour slowly started in the night sky, with the blue being replaced with yellow and then golden orange smears. They watched in awe as the Moai appeared in front of them; first the outlines of the statues standing, followed by their features, as more light came through, and although the sun had not yet appeared, Fanny had lost all interest in food and was taking photographs of the scene in front of her.

Tamika called them over to the water's edge and holding each of their hands said, "I am so happy to meet you, to have chance to be here in this site, and watch the sun rise. I wish you happiness in New Year and I wish that we meet again, so that we can share another experience together. I am already lucky because I met you."

This was all that was needed for the tears to run down Dora's face as she embraced Tamika as well as Fanny.

It was then that the first signs of the sun rising up over the ocean were seen, and Fanny quickly yanked the two up back to the mound, grabbed her phone, her 'selfie' stick and took the photograph which would become iconic for the trip. It showed the three of them, the Moai in the background, the sea and the sun, the sun of the New Year, the thing that heralded new exciting opportunities to come.

"I hope we will meet again," Fanny said to Tamika, and continuing she hugged each woman closer to her, "because we may need to come and visit Japan soon."

With that, Dora looked at her and, yes, the tears started pouring like a washing machine in full cycle.

❀ ❀ ❀

Two days later and they were back at the airport, and Tamika had asked if she could come and say goodbye. The three of them hugged outside the airport building and Tamika handed each of them a small origami bird. "Thank you," she said, "I have such good time with you."

Fanny looked at the small delicate piece of paper that had been converted from a thing which one writes on, to something one appreciates as a piece of art, and smiled. She then had a bright idea and asked that all three of them cup their hands over the next and Tamika's palm hold the two origami birds on the top. The photographs captured this and Dora even stood back and said to Fanny, "Look at what you are producing; you should have been a photographer."

Tamika continued to smile and then said, "You are a photographer."

With their small tokens that would remind them of this island, with its amazing carvings and even more amazing memories that had been created, they boarded the plane bound for Santiago, sad that they were leaving their new friend behind.

And guess what? Yet again, Fanny looked up and said, "I have to think of England!"

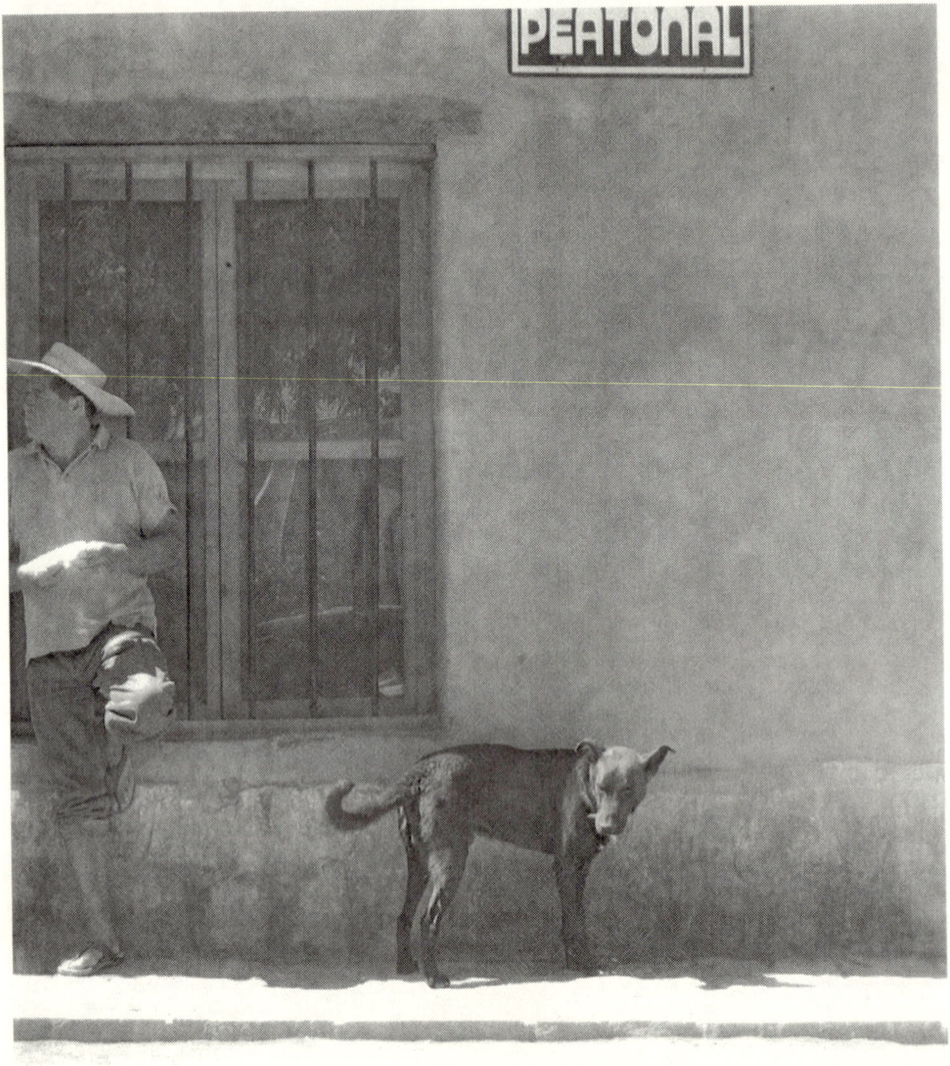
PEATONAL

Part Five ~
Deserts
(wish it could be desserts!)
or simply put:
a place in the sand for the sandman

Chapter Fourteen
Chile
-Santiago

"It is strange to be back in a city again after being on Easter Island," Dora said to Fanny, while sipping her coffee, overlooking the tree-lined avenue.

"Indeed," Fanny replied, "but there is something I wanted to talk to you about."

Dora looked at her with concern, not sure what was coming.

"This holiday feels like a dream to me. Each place we visit is so unique, and then we are off and go somewhere completely different. I thought I wasn't going to like this, but as we continue and as we visit more, I await the next adventure. There is something I want to know though: are you tired?"

"Tired?"

"Well, it's just that we have been going on for weeks now and each place has required my undivided attention and used up a lot of energy. I am a little tired."

"This is not something one has to apologise for," Dora said, "this is hard work. John said the same thing and he is in his prime of youth. This kind of travelling takes it out of you, and maybe we need to slow down a bit and take it easy."

"No, we don't have to slow down, Dora, but thank you for considering this. I think I get so excited about things, but I have walked more in these weeks than I have walked in my entire life. Not to mention I've lived dangerously and been bombarded with so many actions and thoughts, it's fantastic. I am happy but I acknowledge that it is okay to feel a little tired. If I feel it, if it's all a little too much, I promise I will let you know."

"Well Fanny, now that you mention it, think about our activities today; following the 'mural meander' that Tamika suggested and then the walking tour of Central Barrios, we are using a fair amount of energy."

Fanny let out a laugh and Dora looked worried. "I always thought when you visited a city you should do all the sights that were suggested, but here we are, about to walk around the Barrio Bellavista area, going to look at murals people painted on walls as an expression of their creativity; didn't think the tourism police would be happy with all of that!"

They both laughed and stood up from their table to go and see the city's hidden artistic gems.

"I have an idea," Dora said to her.

"Let's take a break and go down on a tour tomorrow, so we can sit back as others do the work. You wanted to see the town of Valparaíso so why not do it as traditional tourists?"

"Are you sure we must go down dear? I like that," Fanny replied and was quickly distracted by the mural in front of her.

"This is the one with Pablo Neruda," Dora said looking down at the information that they had written. The colours were black, blue and grey. Dora watched as Fanny snapped away at the various murals.

"Dora, what I like about this area is that there are different artists with different styles all working side by side. Some works are so detailed and precise while others are rough and comic, but they are all individual and the collective works are beautiful. I can't tell you how many photographs I have taken."

Dora raised her eyebrow and didn't need to say anymore.

They continued to wander through the roughly drawn map and directions that they had received, and while Dora navigated, Fanny snapped away.

"Right then," Dora said, once they were back at their starting point, "we should make our way to Central Barrios to see the more 'formal sites'," and this was followed by a chortle and another until she was holding her sides because she was laughing so much. "And remember when we do our show-and-tell back home, we will have to pretend we started with all the 'formal sites' first!"

That afternoon they wove their way around the Plaza del Armas looking at the buildings which were part of the history of the city. Dora insisted on seeing the Mercado Central with all its fresh food and flowers, but it was when they reached Cerro Santa Lucia that they found that bit of magic, that bit of magic that they had looked forward to.

There were cobbled streets, with interesting walkways and flowers. Fanny bounced about looking for the best angles and shots. When they came to the top, there was Santiago all around them.

"What a way to come to see this," Dora said, but it was lost on Fanny, who was snapping away, focused on ensuring that she use the panoramic function that Tamika had taught her to capture the scene in front of her.

❀ ❀ ❀

"Here's a driving tour of Valparaiso. That's perfect! We can see the city and stop to take pictures at the tourist sites," Dora exclaimed.

"Perfect," said Fanny, looking over the blurb in the pamphlet.

And then, before they even had time to think, because there had been so much happening (in their humble defence), they were booked and sitting on a bus to Valparaiso. It was not one of those where you got off, but rather where they drove you through the streets sharing information about the town.

"Look at all of these colourful buildings," Dora said, "it's going to be exciting."

And for the whole day they sat comfortably in the small bus as it left Santiago bound for Valparaíso.

It wound its way through the streets, stopping at the various buildings before ending up at a restaurant which overlooked the harbour.

The highlight of the day was when they were perched high above the town; there was the beautiful view that postcards were made of. Fanny suddenly thought about the unique photo opportunity, and grabbing her phone, shouted to Dora, "You have to take a photograph right now of me and the town below."

Dora, startled, had taken the phone and looked to see where Fanny was. She had almost leopard-crawled over a very surprised and very worried-looking Japanese tourist who was clutching his own camera, concerned it may be squashed in the avalanche. Fanny stood -- well, kneeled -- in front of the window with her back squashed against it.

"Shoot me, shoot me," she said in what she thought was a Marilyn Monroe voice, but it was actually the voice of an aged drag queen.

"Alright, alright," Dora muttered, peering at the screen in front of her as she heard the sounds of something being slid up and down. She aimed and took the picture and it was only as she looked at it that she realised that Fanny's skirt was showing way above where it should have been. She was flashing everyone behind her, and it was with her rather plump 'bottom.' She quickly motioned to her, by using her hands to gesticulate the problem.

But Fanny continued to speak in her Marilyn voice, "I want to be alone."

Dora could not allow misinterpretation of icons, and had to say, "That was Greta Garbo, and you are flashing your bottom at the people below."

Fanny turned around in fright, and the Japanese man, who clearly had been through enough, quickly exited the row to pretend he needed to take photographs of his own.

What Fanny would not tell Dora was that there was a couple standing outside the window while the whole charade was going on and had clearly seen everything. The woman's mouth was hanging open in disbelief and the man simply stared. She had looked at them both, smiled and even given the man a wink.

With that she was back in her seat next to Dora and the episode had indeed been one she would not forget. Dora had to show her the photograph and they started laughing hysterically, then even more so, until the driver of the bus slowed down thinking one of them was having a heart attack and these howls were in pain. Dora had simply given him a thumbs up and they brought their laughter under control.

"This was once a bustling town," Dora said.

"Yes, I remember reading that," Fanny responded.

"Then the Suez Canal came and changed it all."

"Life is full of ups and downs and changes," Fanny considered.

"Can you imagine telling people that you were going to take photographs with a phone?" Dora chortled.

"One of those big public telephones in the red booths, you know, the ones in which we used to sit and make calls to each other? Well, the young generation have no clue about them. Can you imagine them dragging it behind them as they went about their daily life now?"

With this they were once again in stitches.

"Life."

Chapter Fifteen
Chile
-San Pedro De Atacama

The bus ride had been Fanny's idea. Well more like an idea out of hell. They had been served a ghastly drink which fizzed like a firework on New Year's Eve. They had both smiled and as they both were thirsty, had decided it was now or never.

Fanny, sitting at the window, had held up the drink to the light. It sparkled like an emerald. If it had looked green in the cup, then against the light it was luminous green and looked like what one would expect to see against a wall. A wall belonging to a hippy, not the wall of well…, not against their wall.

They clicked their plastic cups in unison. Dora had turned to say, "If I die as a result of this, I want to donate everything to research into banned and illegal substances." This was followed by the customary chortle. "There is only one way to do this Fanny, drink it down in one shot and hope to hell our travel insurance covers us for this."

With that, they both took a swig and Fanny pretended to make gasping noises much to the distress of Dora, who actually thought it was real.

"I am only joking, silly!" she said, towards a face filled with concern.

"Bloody hell!"

"Oh my word! You've taken my words from my mouth. Doesn't taste too bad, does it?"

"Well no, unless you are addicted to cough mixture," Dora said with a deadpan expression.

"Right then, let's try again."

"Bottoms up, old girl." And with that, the last of the green liquid disappeared.

"Captain, I can't take my liquor," Fanny let out a burp which reverberated through the bus. "Sorry," she said rather sheepishly. But then the laughter was once again ripping through the otherwise quiet bus.

"Well we can see what it does to you," Dora said, "but I am going to be on a sugar high for weeks!"

Fanny looked out the window at the landscape where plants were becoming sparser as they were replaced by the roughness of sand. From the staring, sleep slowly took over and soon she was dreaming about *green aliens, drinking green juice and chasing green humans about.*

When she woke, it was with a start. Dora was prodding her. "Time to go."

"Go where?"

"We are at San Pedro De Atacama."

"You are a what?"

Dora raised her eyebrow and with that, Fanny quickly gathered her belongings and they were outside in the cold night air. There was very little light and the stars looked so close you could touch them.

"Well, time to find the poor soul who agreed to meet us."

They didn't need to look far because there was a most amazingly gorgeous man with a tanned face, jet black hair and piercing eyes (even in the darkness she was able to see this, for the record), with a sign which simply read:

Fanny and Dora

Fanny saw it and did not step forward but simply salivated, "I can be whoever you want me to be."

"You too? He is mine!" and with that Dora gave a little wave at him. Then the smile...well, enough said about that.

Before they knew it, they were meandering through the small streets, which were also like a maze. They were so sad to see him go, as the lady at the reception desk took over.

And with that they drifted off to sleep, with different dreams this time:-

A gorgeous man, with Dora in his arms as he carried her from a burning house.

Aliens chasing people, Fanny's forced into drinking a ghastly-looking green drink and then a gorgeous man who comes and fights them off, with lasers that come out of his eyes.

❁ ❁ ❁

The town was the set of a western movie. There was no way this could have been real. The flat-roofed, shady-coloured houses, the unpaved roads, all of it. This must have been created for tourists, there could be no other reason for this, and that Steven Spielberg man must have had a hand in it.

To prove her point, Fanny looked at a man who was standing against the wall, with his James Dean hat (well, she was not sure if it was a James Dean hat, anyway, with his cowboy-looking hat). He was standing there, just standing there.

Fanny couldn't resist. "I need a photograph of that with me." She winked at Dora.

"Well it's a bit rude to go and ask someone if you can photograph them. Won't it be a bit awkward?"

"Well, we are not going to ask him. I am going to walk past him and pretend I am admiring the streets. Then I will sidle up to him on the other side, where he can't see me, and that is when you shoot. No voices this time!"

"And what if you get caught?"

"We will deal with that, if it happens."

Before anything further could be discussed, Fanny was off looking around the streets, although not too subtly, and if anyone actually saw her, she would have looked like a duck which was in the process of trying to find its younger life. However, to her credit, she did manage to get to her target, which was close to the man. With that, Dora zoomed in and took a photograph of Fanny, smiling as if she had won the Lotto, and cowboy man not moving while a small (well, not so small) person stuck her head out and smiled while clawing at him with her hands.

With a move which almost made her lose her balance she catapulted herself to within metres of the man. He quickly turned around and put out his arms to assist her. Sadly, he was not as successful as he had hoped, as Fanny came crashing into him and both of them landed on the road below. In seconds he was back on his feet, extending his hand to her, muttering in Spanish. He was not quite able to help Fanny completely up, but he at least he allowed her to get her balance back. Fanny pretended that absolutely nothing had happened.

"*Gracias*," she preened.

The man smiled at her and Fanny smiled right back.

Dusty and dreamy, she looked like she was skipping as she made her way to Dora, standing on the other side of the square. There was no other statement than, "Did you get the photograph?"

"Did I get the photograph?" Dora said, sounding like a headmistress.

"Wasn't that exciting? I was able to get closer than I thought to my subject."

"Well let me show you what it looked like from here." Dora showed her photograph after photograph -- what looked like slow motion as Dora had kept shooting and had captured the entire episode, including her crashing into him. The man's face had registered shock, then clearly what looked like being winded by a club that had hit him with full force on his chest, then with more terror as he went crashing to the ground, all while Fanny's hands extended above him. She looked like a love-sick teenager aware that she had done something terrible. The best shot of them all, Fanny's skirt once more above her, looking like an extension of Superman, or Superwoman, and finally the crumpled heap which was the combination of one very squashed man and one very flattened woman with her legs in the air. Fanny watched in awe.

"Well that is a montage which fits right in here in the movie."

Fanny did not know what to say, so simply looked at Dora, and she looked right back, but with a big and very naughty smile.

❋ ❋ ❋

Fanny was in heaven; that was the only way to describe it. She had never envisaged that San Pedro de Atacama would have all these treats and within reach in the road here, only to discover more once you meandered through the town.

As they sat in a restaurant with a bizarrely blazing fireplace next to them they decided to plot their next adventure. Did they go to the Valley of the Moon and Death Valley or did they go and see the El Tatio Geysers? The latter required a swimming costume and sunscreen. This sounded intriguing but they were worried that their scrawny and robust frames may put the tourists off.

So, they decided on the former, and, after all, how exciting Death Valley and the Valley of the Moon sounded. They looked at each other and wondered yet again if that film maker has set these up, as they sounded very exotic.

The next morning they boarded the bus and they were away. The site was not as close as they thought it would be and they bumped and moved for two hours.

And then they both peered with fascination at what lay in front of them. It was indeed like the moon with its craters and landscapes dotted with dunes. They disembarked and wandered around.

"Dora, we can say that part of our travels was to the moon. Can you imagine some of those faces? They are so gullible that I think we should do it. The only problem is that we don't have space suits. Well, let's see how many of them notice that..."

With that Dora was once again the photographer as Fanny bound around the landscape posing, then with her arms outstretched like Neil Armstrong -- well, she was not sure exactly what he looked like -- she rotated and rotated while pictures were taken.

Once finished they continued to walk and very slowly made their way up to a dune which lay out high in the landscape. This was not Valparaiso, considering that there was no colour here, only the sight of sand. There was also no chance of a repeat of Fanny's flashing bottom terrifying the tourists below. Dora let out a sigh of relief.

When they were beckoned back to the bus, they looked one last time over the Valley of the Moon and Fanny said to Dora, "Well, I never thought I would go the moon."

Dora smiled as she slowly started the descent.

They were back in the bus bouncing once more. The landscape was punctuated with the odd plant and Fanny stared dreamily out of the window. This was so different to the manicured gardens of the village, with their flowers placed in precision in their beds.

When Death Valley loomed before them, Dora was expecting to see the landscape littered with bones of humans who had been brought here to die, and she could easily list whom she would bring from the village where they lived! When the doors opened, she could see that hot flushes were nothing in comparison with what was coming through.

This was going to be interesting. It was as if they were going to survive through a furnace. Dora could now understand why it was called Death Valley, because the heat would probably kill you; drowning in your own sweat was the next thing!

This was going to be an extremely quick visit, she decided. She turned to Fanny and said, "No prancing around here, *capiche?*"

"*Kapish?*"

"Well, something like that, I heard it on television once and there was some mafia guy -- oh, never mind..."

They were out for less than a minute and returned soaked through with sweat.

"Un-ladylike I do say," Fanny said, draining the water she had brought with.

On the bus ride back they blasted the air conditioning and both wished they could crawl into the air conditioner and be blasted directly.

They sadly waved good-bye to where they had been, which was a perfect mix of food, interesting adventures and, not to forget, gorgeous men!

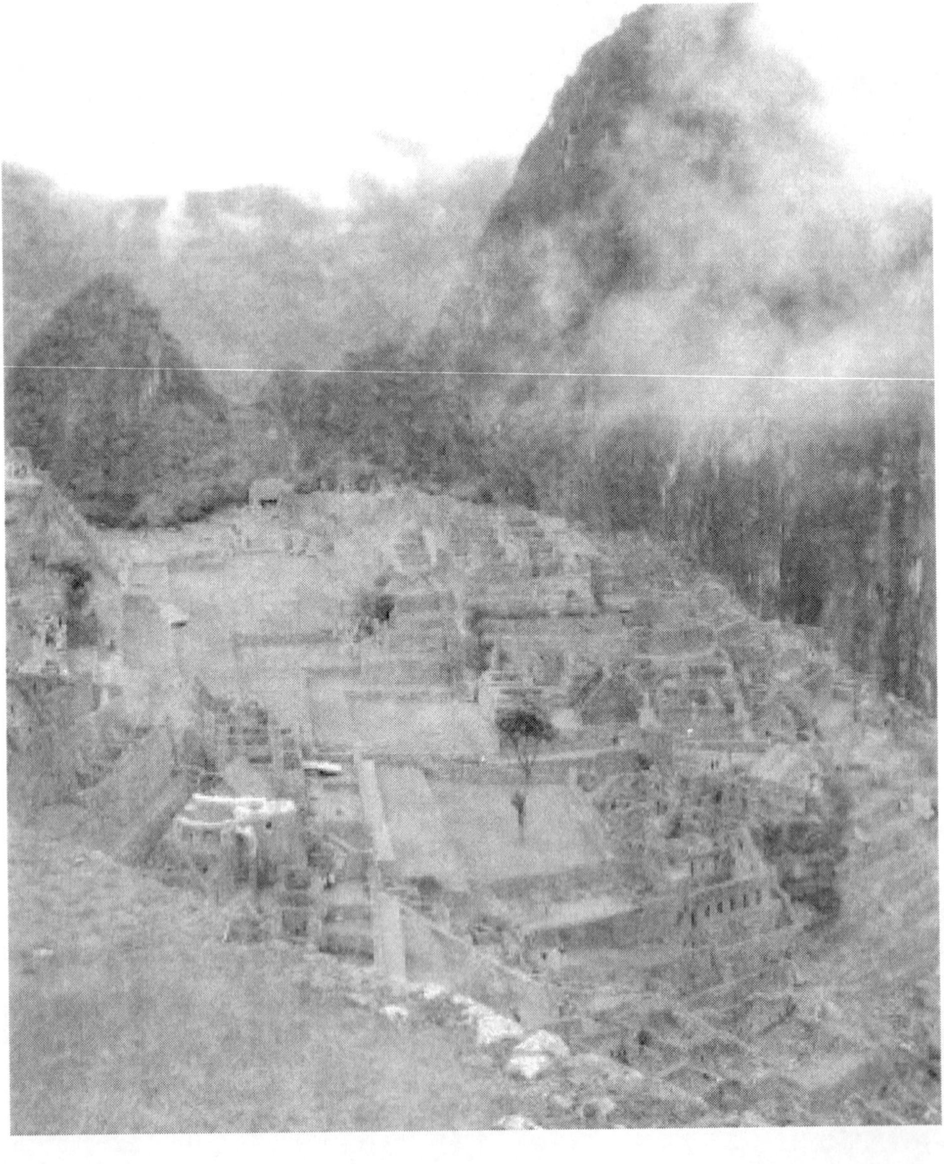

Part Six ~
Lost in time,
or, simply put:
the place at the edge of the Earth

Chapter Sixteen

Peru
-Cusco

"Korikancha," Dora tried to navigate the word while looking at the map of the Inca Temple of the Sun. They would be going on a guided tour and so she was determined to know what each part of the tour would actually cover.

"Listen to this, Fanny," Dora exclaimed. "The original temple used to be lined with golden sheets which reflected the sun. Hope they had insurance!" She laughed at her own joke and Fanny smiled politely as usual.

"Right, then. The temple has been carefully built to align to the sunrise of the June solstice. My word, and they didn't have satellites or any equipment then. Fascinating! Oh, listen to this. There was worship of the Sun God and there was a garden of golden plants. Wish I could have some of those." More snorted laughs. "Yes, even golden corn cobs. Can you imagine the popcorn from that?"

Fanny now joined in the laughter as both of them looked at where this was written in the information booklet. *Golden popcorn!* More laughing, so much so. that like before those around them possibly thought they were drunk.

Once they had their laughter under control, Dora once more read, "There were even twenty life-sized llamas and even a herder to look after them."

This was going to be an interesting tour indeed.

As there was very little of the golden splendour left, they imagined what it could have been like. They meandered through the various sections of the temple and were slightly disappointed that the original temple itself had been covered over time by other buildings.

"Well it's like Bath, or some of the other sites that we have back home; you have to dig to find the treasure," Fanny said.

"Yes, indeed," Dora replied.

Once they meandered through the space, they noticed the beautiful architecture and the almost perfect lines. Fanny was particularly impressed with the gold plate which was from the Incas depicting Mother Earth. On the other hand, Dora liked the contrast of the new church (well, not so new) with the historic site, and she was even heard to say, "Now I see the mixture of new and old and both show the culture from which they came."

Fanny was so shocked by the statement that she wished she had one of those tape recorder things, because this was another rare occasion to note something positive coming out of Dora's mouth.

They took selfies at the curved wall and Dora explained from the information booklet that this is what had survived the earthquake in the 1950's. Both of them looked up, almost expecting the wall to talk back to them. But this was not Israel and they were not at the wailing wall.

❀ ❀ ❀

They were walking though the Convent of Santo Domingo carefully following the instructions they had been given by their guide, a delightful lady who was available to assist them outside. The initial information had Fanny quite concerned. There would be a requirement to be silent for most of the tour. They would be able to hear the odd bit of commentary, but overall this was going to be more on the quiet side. Fanny had no problem with this, but it was Dora who would make the odd remark, and when she did, it was about not agreeing with something.

The walls were painted an earthy red or orange, depending on how colour blind you were. There was a lovely sense of peace as they walked along. They found themselves in a square with colourful flowers everywhere. This is where the guide said, "Next part is working part of convent. We can see many things like the place in which the nuns live. We will be able to go into one, specifically, but please remember that this is a holy site. Let me tell you about the custom here. Once a nun died, they were painted, painted, literally, while they died. If their eyes were open, then it was painted like this, if they were closed then they were painted like that. You can see some examples as we walk around. Please don't go staring at nuns or enter any room."

Fanny didn't know how she felt about the pictures of dead people. After all this wasn't the Valley of Death, and the whole idea of dead people made her tense, ever after watching a film about some child that could see ghosts.

With that, they started walking through the convent and any fears Fanny had were soon replaced with photo opportunities, although never a 'selfie'. The walls, the doors and two signs one which read 'Silencio' and the other which read 'Confessionares". Those were there to remind the nuns of these things, as well as visitors or both. She looked in awe.

It was then that through a doorway she saw a painting of a dead nun. It was not as terrifying as she had originally thought. The face was petite and she had her eyes closed. It was serene. Fanny thought about the artist who would have to spend time with the soul who had just departed and paint it to ensure her memory, as well as meet the deadline of the night.

Then the room in which another nun had lived, the colours and the pictures of the various deities and the most delightful tea set. She had one almost exactly the same as that the one she saw!

When the tour came to an end, the guide who had led them through the convent gave each of them a hug. It was a fitting end to the experience.

What a day they had had, and when they eventually retired for the night, they were ready for their much deserved sleep.

❀ ❀ ❀

Dora rubbed her hands in glee as they set forth on what was going to be an amazing part of their tour. They had been sold a tour to see famous Inca Sites; four to be precise. The man had lured them over to his stand where he had used very animated gestures and words to highlight the tour of the century, something which could easily compare to a visit to Machu Picchu itself.

This was like a dream come true, to be able to walk up the steps of the temple, imagining that she was a sun queen with a python carefully draped over herself. Ascending towards her throne to shout instructions to all those below.

"Yippee," she had exclaimed as Fanny smiled politely next to her. The man also looked very happy that he had such enthusiastic customers.

So there they were, once more in a small bus heading out of the city to the treasures beyond. Dora kept staring out the window, caught up in her thoughts of marching around with her little snake around her neck, while Fanny could only imagine what was a very, very scary sight.

The tour guide spoke over the PA system explaining the history of the various sites they were going to see. He kept repeating himself and Fanny continued to keep up her good spirits and diplomatic face. However, a feeling deep inside told her that something didn't sound right.

"Thiiisss site thought to be military outpost but this cannot be confirmed. And thiiisss one thought to be the temple of water, and thiiisss one military base. And thiiiiisss one a fortress for military or it could be a shrine…"

Fanny was confused because everything sounded like a shrine or a military site. How could they be both? She didn't say anything, but then they pulled up to a parking area and once more the guide said, "This is Sacsayhuman and no one is sure about itsss real purposssseee. It is thought to be a fortresssss or a shriiiine. The carved stones are three hundred tons each."

Some Americans in the front row gasped at this information. Fanny thought, there are all types in this part of the world.

Dora was eager to get out and flung herself out the van in sheer excitement. As they walked past the entrance area, there was a pile of three hundred-ton stones but not in any form like a temple; they were just lying there, kind of dead.

The look on Dora's face was tragic. The light had gone, the dream had died.

Cinderella had left the ball and Sleeping Beauty had woken up. "What the hell…?"

Fanny intervened, knowing where this was going to go, "This must be one of the lesser sites, you know, not every one could be in the state of those we have seen in the magazines."

This did not help to alleviate the disappointment that Dora had and the light had still not come back to her eyes.

They walked through the site and Fanny found herself making clucking noises, just like the Americans had. Dora made no sounds whatsoever and not one word left her lips.

"Well, that was very interesting," Fanny said as they made their way back to the bus.

"Hope you enjoyed the historical site," the guide said.

"Wow, those stones were big," the American said.

No one else said anything and the guide carried on, "The neexxtt site is Puca Pucara thissss site is an interesting one because they do notta know if it was a military outpost or soomeething else."

Fanny could only smile at the unfolding disaster. No sooner were they off the bus and Dora said in a monotone voice, "You have to be kidding me." In front of them were some rocks neatly stacked together.

"Now, now, Dora," Fanny said, "These are historic sites, and we should appreciate them for what they are. It is not every day you can go and see the ancient ruins of the kingdom."

Again there was a stony silence. No more words.

They were soon back in the bus.

"Hope you ennjoyeed that?" Not waiting for an answer, he went straight into, "The neexxtt site is Quenko, which was the site for the worship of fertility."

Dora's mood quickly picked up, and for the first time since her initial disappointment, there was the slight, very slight, glimmer of a smile. They disembarked and Dora, acting like a petulant child, would not go any further, because there in front of them was the same collection of stones supposedly a temple, supposedly a military site. Well, something.

Instead Fanny had found a child dragging a llama about. She cooed and ahhed over this and with her back to her disappointed friend pulled out her camera and took a picture. No sooner had she finished than the child's mother came over and said, "Pay, payy money, payy money for taaakkke picture."

Fanny looked confused.

The mother then took a swipe at the camera and Fanny backed away. Dora quickly fished a note out of her pocket and turned to Fanny and said, "I can't do this anymore!"

"Dora, please."

Dora then marched back to bus without looking at anything further. Slowly the other tourists trickled back and the bus was full once again.

Fanny was worried if the guide asked the now famous question, that Dora might say something awfully rude. Fanny was in luck, because he did not, but went straight into, "The finaaall site is Tambomachay, which is believed to be the thhhee place which was the shrine that was for worship of water." This was followed by a smile.

The journey to the shrine was made in absolute silence. The other tourists were either tired or were also not so happy. Even the American had not said a thing.

They pulled up to the site and Fanny had to pull Dora from her seat to come and see what was outside. There were steps up and there in the distance was water flowing. Dora pulled out her camera reluctantly and snapped a few pictures, while Fanny looked for photo opportunities of her own.

She eventually settled for stones that made some corniche and placed herself firmly inside before taking 'selfie' after 'selfie'. A German girl then told them to go to the drinking fountain because if you drank from it, you would have good luck.

Dora was not sold, but Fanny went over to take part in this ritual. She took a big swig of water and didn't feel much different afterwards. Well, some things maybe took a little bit of time. Dora was already walking back to the bus and that was it.

They arrived back in Cusco and Dora wanted to go and find the man who had sold the tour. She marched through the streets, but then couldn't quite remember where it was. She looked suspiciously at all the men that walked past, hoping to recognise him. She was out of luck because this was not going to happen.

"Come on," Fanny said, "we are going to have some dinner somewhere near the Plaza de Armas."

Dora had possibly realised that she was acting like an insane person, and trotted behind Fanny as they wound through the streets. Eating dinner at a restaurant that overlooked the square Fanny was hypnotised by the yellow taxis which went round and round.

This journey would soon be over, and she leaned to Dora and said, "Tomorrow we go to the place that you and I spoke about so many weeks ago. Tomorrow will be the high point of our travels and I am so excited to be able to have this experience to see Machu Picchu, with you."

Dora smiled back, "Yes, indeed, my new best friend in the whole world."

Chapter Seventeen

Peru
-Machu Picchu

"Fanny!" Dora yelled at the closed bathroom door.

There was a faint response and a murmur which was inaudible.

"I am warning you," she continued, "I will bash down this door, if I have to wait one second more."

Of course, more than one second passed, but Fanny emerged from the bathroom, literally done up to the nines. She had transformed herself and had even powdered her nose and put on some lipstick.

"Where are you going?" Dora enquired.

"Well, one has to look good when one climbs a mountain."

"Well put; hence, I don't think one needs to look spectacularly good to do it. Should we not be wearing hiking boots and have those thingamabobies?" She motioned in the air – it was a mixture of a walking stick and a wand.

"Well you don't look so bad yourself, old gal," came back the rather wicked response.

It was true, they had both prepared themselves for a day that held the promise of a dream come true.

"I guess if we are going on a luxury train -- do you hear that, luxury train? -- One more time, a luxury train -- we can't look like the matrons of a boarding school." The infamous chuckle could be heard.

Fanny smiled, for today, anything would go.

The hotel had organised a car to take them to the station from which the Hiram Bingham Orient Express would depart, and as the streets passed by they made their way to the station. Dora looked like she was going to cry. Fanny placed her hand on Dora's. The humming of the car and the images from outside were their companions.

"Welcome, Madam," the waiter said.

Fanny looked around and was unsure if he was addressing her. Dora did not blink an eyelid as she walked forward and said, "Well, hello there, we are guests who will be travelling by train today."

"Of course, Madam."

Fanny was towing behind Dora and peeked out and noticed the train for the first time. It was painted blue, and had gold lettering on the side. The excitement was infectious. Dora had now also focused her eyes on the splendour in front of her.

Their gaping was gently interrupted with, "Would you like some champagne?"

"Why not?" Dora said in delight.

Fanny gave her friend a cautious look; this was not like Dora.

Before the waiter could even ask Fanny, Dora raised her hands and said, "Champagne, champagne for everyone."

There was silence from Fanny as she looked on in terror.

"My friend Christina always used to say that." Dora looked away, "She is not with us anymore, therefore a fitting celebration of her."

The waiter took this in his stride and prepared the champagne flutes and served them.

"Oh, hell, why not?" This was Fanny's turn to let herself surrender and since the waiter and Dora had been insistent, she convinced herself.

The platform was full of other guests, chatting in their groups, and when it was time to board, they were not herded onto the train as had happened in busses and taxis, no; they were invited, pampered. The gentleman in the train in his oh-so–smart uniform even took their hands as they ascended the step into the carriage.

They were seated in their dining cart and looked at the fine silver napkins which had been laid out in front of them. Dora winked at Fanny as she was beaming.

Dora then conspiratorially leaned forward to ensure that whatever it was would not be heard by anyone else.

"We have to go to the observation car, as I was reading that we have to sit on the right hand side as we leave town to get the best view."

Fanny who had been feeling quite comfortable to this point, now looked down at the silver as the information came dripping over the nice clean napkins. With that, Dora, without saying a word, imitated getting up and motioned to the back of the carriage.

They walked slowly, as Fanny would later find out, so as not to look suspicious and bring attention to themselves. Dora was on a mission; that was quite clear.

The charade continued as they moved into a carriage and it was then that Dora increased her pace and broke out into a very, very, very focused walk. She was walking like those power-walkers who could be seen in those races, or in that funny Central Park in New York City. She smiled at the gentleman who opened the door and was in the process of catapulting herself towards the right hand seat, realising that she was being hotly pursued by a woman who looked like a younger version of herself. Both attempted to get to the prized space. Fanny, realising that she needed to intervene here, because she couldn't just stand there and watch this horror unfolding, intercepted the Dora look-alike by quickly placing her rather large frame in front of her. It was a slow motion moment and yes, Dora won! Fanny rebounded from the quick move and both of them were clearly placed in the spot that they had planned to be.

The Dora look-alike was fuming, smoke coming out of her ears and nose -- well, almost, at least. If looks could kill, they would have been mashed into potatoes. The manic face indicated that this was not going to be the only time when she had taken them on and she was going to get them back; come hell or high water, it looked like there was going to be ongoing conflict. Dora simply turned her back and peered out of the not yet moving train and Fanny followed.

Music started to play behind them and as they turned around, still with their feet stuck to the floor, women in local dress were twirling and dancing in front of them. The Dora look-alike had no choice but to retreat into a corner.

The train started and they were soon gently in sync with the movement of the wheels as they looked out at the city. As it swept past they could understand why this was the best spot, as all the buildings and people loomed up ahead of them. Soon the city was replaced by fields and farmland and they stared out in wonder. Slowly other guests made their way back into the carriages and even the Dora look-alike had disappeared.

The kind gentleman who had welcomed them onto the train now came to fetch them, "Brunch will be served shortly, can I accompany you back to your seats?"

With his arm extended he took Dora's hand, with Fanny feeling a pang of jealousy, and then turned to her and gave the other hand as carefully as he could. *That needs to be stressed* - he gave his other hand and carefully navigated the two of them back to their seats. He made sure that Dora walked in front, he in the middle and Fanny behind! The picture may have looked comic to anyone who could see this carefully choreographed movement, but to them it was heavenly.

Once they were firmly in their seats, once more ensconced in their little piece of heaven, the food descended. And it did not stop. Course after course was placed in front of them and when they thought that there could be no more, another plate appeared out of nowhere. At the end of the meal Fanny fell back against the seat in pure delight.

"I need a paramedic," she pronounced, "I may have died and gone to heaven, again."

Dora quickly responded, "Well that makes two of us, I hope the ambulance is big enough for two." Chortle, chortle.

The countryside continued to fly by and then the train slowed down and they knew they were nearly there. The train stopped and in front of them lay the station, and Dora took in a deep breath.

And then it happened. Neither one was prepared, as the Dora look-alike was on the platform, ready to look at the small shops that littered the station. The Dora look-alike once more stared at them. Dora was not going to take this lying down and stared right back at her. A war of looks had ensued, with neither one going to give up anytime soon. A minute passed by, then another one and then what can only be described as a miracle from a higher power -- A small child tugged on the sleeve of the Dora look-alike and the tension was broken as she pointed to the goods which were on sale in her mother's stall. Fanny, taking stock of the situation, grabbed Dora's arm and they soon disappeared into the maze of delights in front of them.

This was short lived as they were instructed to walk to the bridge by the staff, which was the link to the bus that was going to take them up to the sacred site. Dora walked over it, as if it had some magical power, each step more dramatic than the last. Her hands were not by her sides; instead they were pointed with her palms upward and she closed her eyes with each step. Luckily there were not many who witnessed this.

They were sure to make it to the buses in time for the final drive up the mountain. Luckily for them the Dora look-alike was not in the same bus and Fanny heaved a sigh of relief. Well, that was the last time she would feel relief, because when the bus started up and began to meander the route up, the sharp turns caused her to gasp in shock, each more terrifying than the next. Dora, on the other hand, looked completely calm and unfazed. Then came another rollercoaster moment and Fanny placed her hands against her eyes; she couldn't look anymore. Then the bus halted and Dora once more had to pull her to get out of her trance and to literally help her out.

"Can I charter a helicopter down?" asked a still shaken Fanny.

"It was fun," Dora said.

"If I ever doubted that I need a pacemaker, that was the test."

Their guide warmly welcomed them and explained the tour to them and also pointed to the hotel that they were going to have tea at.

Fanny rubbed her hands in delight, Dora noticed, the terror vanishing very quickly.

"More food," Dora exclaimed, emphasising 'food'. There was no subtlety in her words.

"Can never have too many hats, shoes, bags, champagne and food," was the response.

"Well put," Dora said, smiling at her friend.

❀ ❀ ❀

"Machu Picchu means 'old mountain' in Quechea language. I hope you are ready to see one of the most amazing sights in the world. I see it every day of my life and every day I feel the same, this is a footprint of the Gods. I now say the famous words of Haram Bingham, "In the variety of its charms and the power of its spell, I know of no place in the world which can compare with it."

Dora stood mesmerized by these words. There was a tear, a single tear which slowly moved down her face, past her cheek, her chin and then onto the floor. It represented something which Fanny would not be able to understand or comprehend. One thing she did know was that this must have been something which Dora had longed for. It was the very thing that she had started with in her very explanation of the need to go to South America. It was going to the last place they would visit. She gently touched her shoulder and squeezed.

"How silly of me," Dora said self-consciously.

"That is not silliness, that is beautiful, and you are amazing."

Dora did not have to say anymore and looked at her friend with gratitude.

"The site was completely hidden from below and was able to sustain itself without a need to be engaged with anything below. It had agricultural terraces on which the inhabitants were able to grow crops for consumption by the populace. There are 150 houses, to give you an idea of how many people lived here." The guide's voice rang out over the mountains.

"This was also primarily used as an astronomical observatory. Enough of me talking. Please follow me," he said, and then he slowly moved them around the side of the mountain.

"Right, it is time for you to see Machu Picchu," and with that, he stepped aside and there below them lay the iconic image which had been brought to life. Most of the tourists gasped and Fanny realised she had too. Dora had not made a sound; she stood transfixed, staring below. Her head moved slowly as she viewed the site slowly from one side to another.

Fanny, eager for Dora not to say something inappropriate about it being a collection of rocks, decided to distract her. "We need a selfie, don't we?"

"Please give me a minute," she whispered, her eyes still absorbed with the prominent site.

Dora finally shut her eyes, stood still and took a deep breath.

There was not elation, or disappointment; there was a Dora she had never seen. A Dora stunned by a moment caught in time. Fanny knew she didn't have to do anything, but she would do whatever Dora wanted, because this was her time. She was in a trance, a trance of reverie.

When she was ready, she stood next to Fanny and said, "Fire away! This is a moment I will never forget as long as I live." And with that, up went the selfie stick, and they both smiled in delight. When they looked at the picture, there was nothing else that was needed, for it captured both of them, elated.

There above Machu Picchu was Huayna Pichcu. It towered over the site, and as Dora looked at it she pointed to Fanny, "Look how majestic it is. The clouds have surrounded it, to protect it from us." Chortle.

And although the guide had mentioned the restrictions, both of them had decided that this was not the time to go hiking, especially if Fanny were to faint and fall on some other climbers on the way down.

Once they reached the site below, Fanny and Dora followed the guide's advice and decided to explore the three areas and assemble back, to hear more of the history.

Dora, clearly in her element, started walking in circles.

"Dora, whatever is wrong with you?" Fanny asked with concern.

"I don't know where to go first; the religious section, the residential section or the agricultural section."

This seemed to be a real conundrum that Dora was facing, so Fanny decided to intervene.

"Well, shall I decide then?" she didn't wait for a response, "even if they are not in order, why don't we go to agricultural first, then go domestic and end with the religious. This will ensure that we are left with the memories of the spiritual connection."

"Fanny," it was said slowly, and Fanny was prepared for the rebuke, "you are a genius! You have made it so easy. That is exactly what we will do."

"Right then, you know where to go," Fanny had not even finished her sentence when Dora was already aiming them towards an open field.

They trundled along, and then Fanny knew why this was called the agricultural area. As the guide had mentioned, there were terraces on which various crops were planted.

"Look at that," Dora said, marvelling at the carefully kept terraces, which had been almost systematically placed, one below the next. "Are you up for a brief climb?" Dora enquired.

Fanny didn't even need to be asked, and said, "Let's do it."

Dora continued to make sounds as they walked up, and they were able to marvel at the stone structures closer. Up and up they went until they reached what looked like the top.

"I was keeping this as a surprise," Dora said mischievously. "We have ascended the steps to heaven. I hope that is the case…" Fanny looked perplexed, something which did not happen often. "Well, today, even if they are not really the steps to heaven, it feels like we have just ascended them." And with that, she turned around and made a humming noise. "Well, you know what, both of us are really close to getting there, so we should look carefully at what heaven looks like."

It was Fanny this time who let out a loud laugh. "Well as you said, these are the steps to heaven, so technically we are in heaven, even if we are still alive. That will take some explaining to that lot back at home." So began the descent from heaven back to the mere mortals below.

The domestic site allowed them to go inside the structures that made up the various houses. Fanny stood and considered what it must have taken to build these.

"Think about it, Dora," she said. "There were no hardware shops, or cranes or scaffolding; there were just people moving around fifty-tonne rocks. They must have had help from the gods above, as there is no way they would have been able to do it." This was worrying her and she could feel the tensing of her brow.

"That is exactly what I was thinking. I think of Bob the Builder who does most of the work in building in the village. He struggles to pick up the cement bag, let alone those brick pallets. And he moans about how hard it is," Dora also looked irritated. "And he has the audacity to complain. Just wait until I tell him about what we have seen here. No more moaning…or else!"

The stone structure Dora touched (although she remembered reading somewhere that she should not do this, she couldn't help it) held a history to it; hundreds of years of history. If these walls could talk -- was it asking too much for them to do that? -- and then she chortled, much to the confusion of Fanny.

Fanny, on the other hand, was convinced that Dora was finally the victim of some old person's syndrome. Poor thing; well, at least she had realised her dream of seeing Machu Picchu.

"Move along, Fanny," the instruction was issued, "we need to go and witness the majesty of the religious space. As you said, this is what we should end with."

Dora knew more about this site than any guide. "It is here, here at the Intihuatana stone, the 'Hitching Post of the Sun', that the two equinoxes take place, one in March and one in September. It is when the sun lies directly over this site. When the sun 'Sits with all his might on the pillar' and is 'tied' to the rock. How magnificent is that beautiful, poetic description?"

"Did you know all of that yourself?" Fanny enquired, dumbstruck.

"Of course not, it comes from a book. Now to carry on," Dora said, flustered.

Fanny knew that any more questions were not part of this visit.

"Now, the denouement: they tied the sun to the rock. They did this so that it would not be able to move northwards." Dora had her right hand in the air and, pointing with her index finger, indicated where north was. There was silence.

Fanny wondered if she should ask what the final part was, as Dora had said denouement, and yet, there was nothing with which to explain the climax and subsequent end. No point in crying over spilt milk.

"That is impressive," Fanny exclaimed, "but what is even more extraordinary is that you were able to remember and bring to life the story behind this inspiring monument to the sun."

Dora smiled shyly, not expecting the praise.

It was then that Fanny said to her, "Now, I am going to say something and I don't want to be judged. It's a bit like that movie *Ghostbusters*."

"Well, you just had to endure my performance."

"It's that I feel something here," Fanny started, "not only because we are in the religious part of the site. I feel an energy, the electricity of a spirit that surrounds me, excites me, and yet also makes me feel content. It is hard to describe, but there is something here."

"There is an energy here. I would describe it differently to you, but we both feel something. I feel an emotion, I feel sadness, I feel a contented peace. I feel that these stones hold secrets and stories that will never be released. I feel that I will be infected by Machu Picchu for as long as I live."

"Well…, that is exactly what I feel, but you are the one who has the way with words."

"I have to ask you a favour," Dora said quietly.

"Anything you want."

"Can we go and sit over there and absorb the atmosphere, feel the energy, simply be?"

"Sounds like a perfect way to end our visit."

It was when they were firmly sitting side by side that the whole trip flashed before Fanny's eyes: The wonders of Brazil and the museum of Carmen Miranda, the tango of Argentina, the gorgeous man of San Pedro de Atacama, the marvels of Easter Island and here, where they sat, where they could truly appreciate what it was to be human. Fanny let out a deep sigh. This was absolute contentment.

Dora had also been thinking. Life was about opportunity but really it was possibility and dreams. It was a way to experience that which could be. Not everyone would have the chance, but while she could, she had done something that had once lain as a seed inside her, that had slowly germinated and grown, and this was it; she was here today. She had transformed her friendship from a superficial everyday one in which you drank tea and moaned about the weather, into a cave of gratitude, a place where she could not only have a friend, but truly live through that friend. See the world through someone else's eyes and be, with some judgement, but mostly she had been allowed to free herself, knowing that she would always have that friend to fall back on.

"Fanny," Dora said, choking up, "all I can say is, thank you. Thank you for coming with me on this journey. I could never have dreamed that we would have seen what we did, experienced what we experienced…I am truly thankful."

Fanny could not say anything, because if she did, there was no doubt that the tears would come pouring -- no, that is not enough -- would come flowing out. She was also choked up and she reached across and gave Dora the biggest hug she had ever given another soul.

Both continued sitting and staring out at the vista above and below them. Neither of them needed to speak, because this was truly the culmination of their trip and no words would be able to describe it.

The rest went by in a flash, definitely because it involved treats for tea, so Fanny was in her element. Arriving back at the bus with more drama and Fanny yelping at each turn, the scented towels awaiting them before the train, the Dora look-alike seated directly next to them and this time Dora greeting her and apologising for her actions… Then Dora and Dora look-alike both drinking a Pisco Sour (although I really believe this an unfortunate name for a drink), Fanny believing that the world was coming to an end, for this was impossible, her eyes must have been deceiving her; Dora had never apologised to an enemy. Fanny taking a photograph of both of them, the train trip back, Dora mentioning that she felt like a stuffed peacock. The night journey lulling them both into thought, packing and Lima, and finally, boarding a flight home.

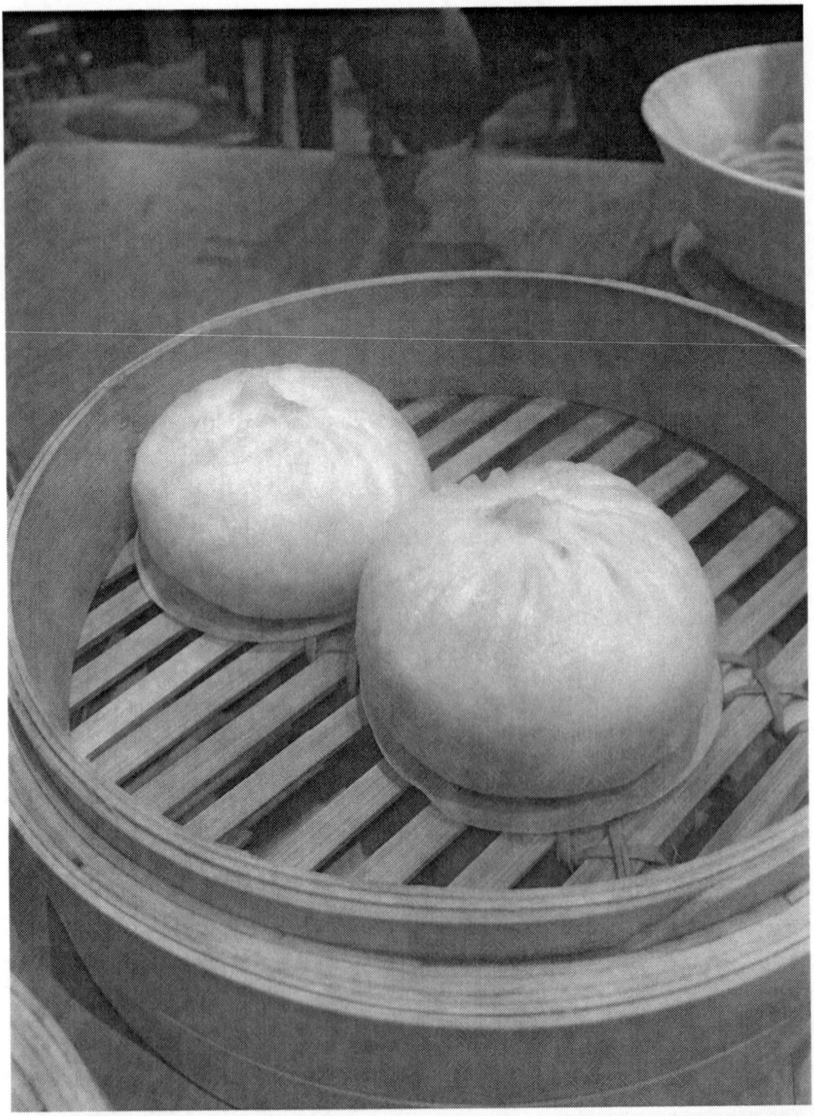

Part Seven –
The end of time,
or, simply put,
the end!
(Not quite!!!)

Chapter Eighteen
Country Location UNKNOWN!!! (Right?) No! Country Location KNOWN!!!

Does plane count as a little village? No, it counts as a time machine, or a magic carpet!

And now they were perched in their seats, the last few days feeling like the whirlwind that they were. There were no Pisco Sours, or champagne, for that matter. Dora wanted to write to the airline and complain, as this was not cricket. Fanny reminded her that she had turned a leaf and so would no longer behave like that.

"Dora, it is my turn…"

"For what, dear?"

"It is my turn to say something about this experience. Thank you for bringing me here. Thank you for awakening my soul to the wonders of this world. I was on my way to being the most boring spinster in the history of the world. If they ever made a documentary about spinsters, I would have been lauded as the most spinstery of them all. But that has changed. I thought you were mad when you came to visit me and tell me about what we were going to do. I was hoping that it was a phase you were going through, but it wasn't, and before I knew it, we were bound for South America. Dora, look what you have done for me."

"Is it bad dear? Have I done something bad?"

"NO! You are amazing! You are like a firecracker that has blasted me out into an adventure! You have made me laugh, you have made me lust after a man in a sandy street in Chile. Think about these things."

Chortle, chortle.

"I want to say thank you again. Thank you for being the most amazing friend, travel partner, human being in all the universe. If it wasn't for you I would not feel like I had ascended from the earth to the gods and peered down at the beauty that is this planet."

It was another hug, a difficult one, because of those damn airline seats, but it was a hug nevertheless.

And with that, Dora once again turned to her and asked: "Where are we going next?"

"SOOUTTTHHH EEASSST ASSSIIAAAAA," rang across the cabin and then into the night.

And with that, they, and the plane, disappeared into the sunset -- yes, literally!

The End...

Acknowledgments

There are many people to thank who inspired this novella, however, there is not enough time... However, (yes, I know you have seen this word in the sentence prior to this one but -- I like it!!!) I would like to say that I would like to thank my parents who provided me with the wonderful opportunity to be a writer.

Number two, I would like to thank my dearest Rose who has been the greatest, greatest, greatest editor on this project.

And of course, I would like to thank myself because I am amazing !!!

✾✾✾✾✾✾✾✾✾✾✾✾✾✾✾✾✾✾✾✾✾✾✾

Oh, sherbet. I forgot some people! Oh dear! Horrible! Horrible!

I guess I should say a big thank you to -
Mrs Christopher Moller because she did in the end try and read the book, didn't she?

A huge thank you to Miss Priscilla Anthony who was the very first navigator of the story.

Last but not least, I am sending lots of love to Hoon, Elvis and Tina.

And let's not forget Ella Fitzgerald and of course Petula Clark.

About the author: -

Lilibeth Llewelyn Rhys-Davies

Lilibeth has written more books than Westlife has recorded albums. She is glamour personified and respected more than is humanly possible and more than any dictator in the entire world. Everyone wants to read her books!

Jason le Grange

Jason has written more amazing books than singer Enya has recorded albums. He is glamour personified and respected more by extraterrestrial aliens than is humanly possible.

Everyone wants to read his books! Everyone, yes EVERYONE!

www.jasonlegrange.com